Skullface Boy

by

Chad Lutzke

Print edition
Copyright © 2018 Chad Lutzke
ALL RIGHTS RESERVED

This is a work of fiction. Names, characters, business, places, events and incidents are either the products of the author's imagination or used in a fictitious manner. Any resemblance to actual persons, living or dead, or actual events is purely coincidental.

Cover design by Chad Lutzke using the photography of Chas Bacon

To join my VIP reader list and be included in all future giveaways, visit www.chadlutzke.com

Dedicated to the bullied, the parentless and the unique.
May the shallow assholes one day envy you.

1 - So, One Night I Left

My name is Levi. I'm 16. I've got a skull for a face. And here's how shit went down:

Soon after I was born, my mother left me in downtown Denver—*almost* on the steps of Gramm Jones Foster Care. Almost. Closer to the dumpster than to the door. I lived at Gramm Jones for sixteen years. That's a long time. That's not how the system usually works, but that's how it worked for me.

Soon after what they figured was my 16th birthday, Sister Jude encouraged me to leave Gramm Jones, to explore the world. She even dug out my social security card and birth certificate and gave them to me. She knew as well as I did that I'd never find a home. I'd be stuck in there while the world went on without me.

So, one night, instead of daydreaming about it—a habit I'd had for years—I left. I grabbed a backpack loaded with nothing but my favorite book, *The Painted Bird*—good ole' Kosinski sure could make a boy feel a lot less lonely—and walked out the front door in the middle of the night. I think the staff even saw me leave. They just never asked where the hell I thought I was going, like they would any other kid. I'll bet they smiled, lifted their hands in prayer and gave a little thanks that the kid with the skull face wasn't their problem anymore.

That night, I walked by Sister Jude's apartment. It was on the same block, next to the church. I wanted to thank her and say goodbye. I peeked in her window, not because I knew the only pair of tits I'd ever see were through a pane of glass, but because I couldn't bring myself to knock on the door, tell her I was leaving. She'd been the only one to ever look past my face and see the me inside. Being colored, I think she could relate. She'd had her own share of bullshit.

She was on her couch reading a paperback. I couldn't tell which book but knew it was something good. Sister Jude was smart and cultured. I can't imagine she'd lend her time to pages that weren't worth her time.

If I could cry, I suppose I would have. It seemed like an appropriate thing to do at the time. I had no idea if the world had any Sister Judes left or if it was full of the same heartless souls found at Gramm Jones. But I was about to find out.

I waved outside the window, knowing she couldn't see me. The wave was for me, I guess. Not her. Then I headed down East Colfax—the only other street I'd ever walked down.

2 - Shallow Assholes

I've gotten used to my face, but it's a distraction for others. It sticks out in a crowd and is whiter than an Irishman's ass. Bone white. That's my attempt at humor. It's dry humor. Bone dry.

If you can't laugh at the worst then you end up a miserable sack of shit.

When someone gives me the time of day, an actual conversation, they ask the same question: *What happened?* I give them all the same answer: *It ain't important.* The answer never satisfies, and most times the conversation ends there. Could be I come off as abrasive—so I've been told. But most times it's because they're shallow assholes. They never wanted to get to know me. It's all about their curiosity.

Once a kid asked me why I don't just kill myself, jump out a window. See? Shallow assholes.

3 - Moles

East Colfax, particularly at night, holds quite the tribe. Your usual husks waiting around to die. Drugged, drunk, and suffering, mostly by their own hands. It's sad. Especially the ones who just need a leg up, the ones who are there because they followed orders on foreign land, were told they were doing some good. Those are the ones who really get to me. Sometimes I wonder if I went off and killed a bunch of people, saw my buddies get splattered every which way, if I wouldn't turn to medicating myself, too. What I'm saying is, who made who?

Though my view of the world comes only from the books I've read and movies I've seen, Colfax didn't seem that far off from what I'd read in *Junky*. Burroughs would have you think that heroin is on every street corner in every city, but I knew better. I knew cities were a hybrid of the good and the bad. Most of them wanting to be good, to be a safe haven for those who live there, but with an ugly mole right in the middle of it. Sometimes those moles are larger and uglier than others. I learned that places like Detroit and Cleveland and Stockton were mostly mole, festering wounds with little to offer.

I imagine it'd be hard to live in a place like that—high crime, riddled with sin as Sister Jude would call it. The funny thing is, when I'd read the books, the ones with crime and drugs and homelessness and poverty, I found them exciting, not bleak or somber. To me there's nothing more dismal than normalcy or quiet, country living. The city sounds through my window at Gramm Jones are the only thing that kept me sane through the years—a steady heartbeat created by horns, sirens, chatter, and screeches, all reminding me I'm not alone, that there's life out there being lived.

Gramm Jones was a prison sentence. A decade and a half of the same walls, looking out the same dirtied windows knowing damn well wasn't anybody coming for me.

I left without a penny in my pocket or even a change of clothes. Just the backpack, the book, and a headful of everything I ever learned from music, movies, and most of all, books. We're not talking after-school reading. We're talking shitting, eating, and drinking books. You'd be surprised how much you can learn about life when hands-on experience is traded for an embarrassing amount of words read and films viewed.

4 - The Indian I Practiced On

The first person I ran into was at a bus stop, right there on East Colfax near the Capitol building—a beautifully enormous structure that had government written all over it—a four-story beast with pillars and ridiculously wide stairs, all topped with a gold-laced dome that stuck out like the gaudy tooth of a gangster.

The bus stop was the kind enclosed in tinted glass with a bench inside to keep people out of the rain, or to sleep in. A man lay stretched out inside, chanting something tribal. His ink-black hair was matted, bunched together like there could have been a bird's nest in it. Small bits of leaves and lint clung to it—decorations on a burnt Christmas tree. His cheekbones and forehead gave away his Indian heritage. That and the rhythmic howling. It was hard to say how old he was. Could have been 40, could have been 85. His face was rough and split like mudcracks in auburn clay.

I watched the man, hoping he wouldn't see me. I'm not sure why. Heading out into the world I was bound to have human interaction and I needed the practice. I guess I didn't feel prepared.

And then the Indian caught a glimpse of bone. "Holy hell, boy. What happened to you?"

Shit like that was going to be my biggest challenge. Not the eating out of dumpsters or sleeping in parks, but dealing with the reminders. They'd be constant. I wanted to ignore the guy and walk away, but I couldn't pussy out. Not already.

"It's who I am. You don't like it, don't look at it."

The man was stunned silent. My words were blunt. Maybe too blunt. I said I was smart, well read, not that I had social skills.

"What's that, your Colfax talk? You don't gotta front with me, boy. I know damn well that ain't the first time you've been asked that."

I stopped walking, decided to practice on him.

"Sorry," I said.

"You look like you're going someplace but aren't quite ready. You got a cigarette?"

"Nope."

"A dollar?"

"No."

"You even from around here?"

"Been here my whole life."

"Was gettin' a tourist vibe. I saw you marveling at the sights."

"Just looking at it with different eyes I guess."

"Gotchya." The man started humming a little.

"What can you tell me about this bus?" I asked.

"Bus runs through here every half hour. Or every twenty minutes if you're a bad luck bastard who's runnin' late for work. Where you headed?"

It was a good question.

One day Sister Jude told me she used to live in Hermosa Beach, California. She said when she was about ten she'd seen someone like me on the beach, surfing—plaster-white bone with long blonde hair, bleached by the sun. She said she saw him a few times. He'd be surfing early in the morning, always kept to himself.

I wanted so bad to believe that someone out there was just like me that I never bothered to ask her any questions. I was afraid if I dug too deep that I'd find out it was just a lie—a story to keep me optimistic about life, something to give me hope. But really I knew better. Sister Jude wasn't like that. She wouldn't candy coat, and she'd never bullshit me. She even used that very word once, and that's how I knew I could trust her. Also because of the time I slapped a kid, knocked him off his chair during lunch. He'd been flicking my forehead, getting a kick out of the sound it made against his fingernail. I got into a lot of trouble that day, and Sister Jude told me that wasn't anybody gonna hold my hand through life and that I needed to have thicker skin or I'd get eaten alive. I wasn't sure what she meant at the time, but I figured it out.

Yeah, she wouldn't bullshit me. There probably was someone out there like me, someone who thought they were alone, too.

"I'm going to California," I told the man.

"For a brand new start?...and with an ache in your heart?"

I wasn't sure what he meant. Then he kinda chuckled and said, "I can't tell if you're confused or happy or sad, or even awake."

"You're an asshole." I told him. It just came out. I don't think I'd ever said that to an adult before. I've thought it, just never said it.

"Hey now, I think you need to work on your people skills."

"No...I think *you* do. You think I don't know what the hell I look like?"

The guy just looked at me, then he showed me a bottle wrapped tight in wrinkled paper bag. "Want a drink?"

"I'm sixteen."

"So...might do ya some good."

"No thanks."

"So, really. Why you going to California?"

"I'm going to find…"

"A girl with flowers in her hair?"

I shut my mouth, wasn't sure I could have a conversation with the guy, and had no real reason to tell him where or why I was headed.

"Relax, kid. I'm just gettin' the Led out. But I suppose you wouldn't know anything about real music...too busy listening to that garbage." The man nodded at my shirt. That's when I realized he'd been reciting lyrics.

I looked down at my chest and wondered if he'd take me serious if I hadn't made the shirt myself. Or if he just didn't like KISS altogether.

We weren't supposed to wear shirts like that at Gramm Jones—with bands on them—so Sister Jude snuck me a big black marker and I made my own. It wasn't much, kinda shitty, actually. Just the logo with the trademark lightning bolt S's, and I'd glued some silver glitter around the letters like the iron-ons from the 70s. Below the band's name I drew Ace Frehley's spaceman makeup. Just the eyes, and more glitter. I related to the spaceman most—a man not of this world.

As far as music goes, KISS was about all I listened to at Gramm Jones. I'd grown to love the band and the personas they took on, wishing I could be like that, to have people stare at me in awe and envy instead of fear and disgust. The lyrics were juvenile. I get that. Nothing deeper than a child's nursery rhyme, really. But I was never one for poetry with any kind of depth. Literature was different. I read the classics, the Hemingways and Fitzgeralds, the Poes and Shelleys, but I liked to keep my music simple. I liked the dumb downed simplicity of songs about girls and ego and the rock and roll lifestyle. They made life seem brighter than it was, like every bit of it should be a party filled with things like sex and fame and guises. KISS did that well. I collected all those tapes, right up until a few years ago when their makeup came off. I pretended that never happened. It felt like betrayal.

"Ain't nothing wrong with KISS," I said.

"Well, if you're a little punk like yourself, I suppose not."

I ignored the guy. Part of me wanted to spout off about literature and make the guy feel small and insignificant, flaunting my book knowledge and shine a light on him wasting away in the mole of Denver, part of the problem. But I didn't know his story, and I didn't set out in the world to be a dick. I set out to live. No bullshit.

5 - Handouts

I'm not sure why I asked the Indian about the bus. I had no money to ride it, not even to the next stop. But I didn't worry about travel. It was June. More than enough time to get west before the cold hit. With no real plan, I envisioned me hitchhiking out of Colorado, across Arizona and through Southern California, plenty of walking in-between rides. Probably more walking than riding.

That first night, I decided it'd be best to get some sleep, keep my same schedule. I'd get rides during the day and it'd be easier to find a place to crash after the sun went down, knowing most of the time I'd have to hide where I slept. So I walked west down Colfax and stopped at a gas station, got some directions to the nearest highway. I liked the idea of places being open 24/7. It's like the city was always awake and wanting to help, whatever the hour.

The cashier pointed which way to go, told me to hit South Colorado Boulevard and keep going until I ran into a cluster of on/off ramps, said I couldn't miss it. I told him thanks, and he stopped me before I left. He asked me if I wanted the rest of the pizza. He said it'd been sitting under the heat lamp all day and was gonna throw it out. I took a few pieces and asked if I could have some water.

He went and grabbed a large Styrofoam cup and filled it with ice and water, then struggled with the lid, trying to use only one hand. I was about to ask if he needed help, but then saw one of his arms was like an empty sleeve. No bone. No muscle. It hung loosely at his side like a jacket waiting to be pulled on all the way. He finally sealed the cup and handed it to me. I walked out wondering if I looked like someone who was down and out and needed a free meal, or just someone who really loved pizza. I wondered if this was how life was gonna be now. Handouts. I decided for now I guess it'd have to be.

6 - Evergreen Cocoon

While walking down Colorado Boulevard, eating dry pizza with overcooked cheese that stuck to my teeth like wax, I thought about sticking around Colorado, getting a job somewhere for a while until I got enough money for a bus ticket, maybe ditch the whole hitchhiking thing. But with no place to stay, employment seemed like an impossibility. So I stuck to the initial plan, which was no plan at all, other than shortening the distance between me and Hermosa Beach.

I threw the last bit of pizza crust in the gutter along the street. It cracked against the cement, louder than it should have, like I'd thrown a rock. Honestly, the pizza wasn't any worse than what I'd eaten at Gramm Jones. Maybe even better.

I hung onto the cup until I saw a garbage can up ahead outside a restaurant. The restaurant was closed and I caught my reflection in the darkened, wall-like windows. Blue and white lights painted my face, the occasional headlight flashing brightly on bone. I looked at the reflection of my shirt. *SSIK*. A disturbing irony. A dozen brake lights from the intersection nearby burned everything red. My face an angry skull, rage filled. The attraction in a funhouse. The genesis of a child's ritualistic checking under the bed before sleep. I kicked the giant window, trying to break through but hoping I wouldn't. The pane bounced and boomed but stayed intact. The horror in the window turned back to blue and white. It was a weak moment. I have them.

***

I walked for half an hour before spotting the highway. The occasional car would drop in or out of the curved roads that led into or out of Denver. Each circle of road surrounded a well-groomed acreage of grass peppered with bushes and small trees—pleasant mini parks in the middle of chaos. It was beautiful. Streetlights illuminated the spots brightly, while the foliage cast dark shadows, allowing small safe havens from the light. I'd be sleeping there.

I made my way into the shadows between a group of bushes, a small courtyard. I was invisible from passersby but could see the overpass above clearly, Denver's nearby buildings towering high only blocks away. I gazed at one building in particular. It was at least a dozen stories tall, with the top surrounded in a brilliant blue light with words that read *Writers Center*.

I read the words over and over, contemplating their meaning. They prompted an urge to put pen to paper, something I'd always wanted to do but never did. At that moment I decided to write, and if it meant stealing a pen and writing on napkins until they bloated my backpack, then that's what I'd do.

The blue light was calming, and the sound of traffic helped contribute to my now tranquil mood, as the evergreens cocooned me. Tonight's bed. It felt like my first night on a new planet. There was sadness and confusion and fear, and finally, contentment. Every night before that night was me trapped in a cursed womb that neither invited nor welcomed me, just tolerated me. I watched the blue light until I drifted into sleep—the whirring of tires around me, my lullaby.

I dreamt of writing and saving the world with my words, of saving myself. And it was the first time I can remember thinking how it must feel to wear a smile on your face.

7 - This Ain't No Holiday Inn

I woke to a sharp pain in my leg.

"Hey! Wake up, bum."

A guy stood over me, a dirty orange vest hung loosely over a shirt that held the fading image of an eagle. The guy couldn't have been more than twenty-five. He had one of those sticks with the nail-like ends for picking up trash. He'd been poking me with it.

"This ain't no Holiday Inn."

He wanted to poke me again. I sat up, pulled my backpack close to me.

"Ain't no beauty sleep gonna help you, kid. Get up."

The guy didn't strike me as anyone with authority, what with his white-trash shirt and all. I looked down the highway. There were a few other guys like him, picking up trash. A large black man stood against a city truck reading a magazine. These other guys were out here working off community service, a bunch of hoodlums narrowly escaping time behind bars.

I thought about playing stubborn, putting up a fight about how I didn't have to go anywhere. But I needed to start the day, maybe hunt down some breakfast.

I stood near the circled off-ramp, deciding which way was west. Before I hit the highway I figured it best if I got a belly full. Once I got on the highway I'd be miles from food. And getting a ride was no guarantee.

I made my way up the off ramp and headed south down Colorado Boulevard until I saw a McDonald's. I'd hit the dumpster, see if I could find a sealed burger, maybe a Big Mac that wasn't supposed to have mayo but did. There ain't a burger joint in the world that don't toss perfectly good food out on the regular.

I went inside first to get some napkins. I didn't forget that I meant to write. The *Writers Center* and its beautiful blue light, that wasn't just a temporary spell I was under. I was serious about writing, and it'd start today.

I walked to the counter and asked a pimple-faced girl for a stack of napkins and a pen. It was a strange request, so I got a strange look. Or maybe she was a shallow asshole. She handed me some napkins and grabbed a pen from under the counter. I told her thanks and said "I can't bring this back, hope that's okay."

"I guess," she said.

I could tell she hadn't said much all morning because her lips tried sticking together when she spoke and "I" came out like "mi." She blushed and the rest of her face matched her teenage blemishes. I was embarrassed for her. It's times like that I'd offer a smile if I could.

8 - The Freedom I Felt

I was able to find a chicken sandwich in the dumpster. It was wrapped, looked untouched, but had nothing on it. Just chicken and oil-soaked bread. I needed it to tide me over for the next few hours on the highway, then maybe score something better. Still, rides weren't a guarantee.

After I made it back to the highway, I headed west. I didn't try and hitch a ride, not yet. I was nervous, but more so I wanted time to take it all in—the freedom I felt. Me against the world, the road under my feet. No more Gramm Jones up my ass.

The road ahead was vast. This wasn't a dirty window I was looking through. This was the naked world. It was hard to distinguish anxiety from excitement. I felt them both. A belly full of jumping beans. To not know what lay ahead thrilled me. Whatever was ahead didn't matter, so long as it happened outside those brick walls, with the same view of First Place Pharmacy, Stonehill Apartments, and the trees that blocked the playground at Lawndale Elementary. The ones that obstructed my view of the children experiencing their own kind of freedom on that playground. I came to develop a gratitude for those trees. Watching those kids would have been torturous. Listening to their laughter was bad enough.

9 - Confessional

After two hours of walking, taking it all in, reveling, I stuck my thumb out. Hundreds of cars passed. Every one of them saw me, saw my thumb. Saw my face. I walked for two more hours before someone picked me up. It was a middle-aged woman in a pantsuit. She didn't seem the type to be messing around with hitchhiking strangers, but she was.

She made me sit in the back while her snow skis rode shotgun. It was awkward. Other than telling her I was heading as far southwest as I could get, it was quiet between us for the first half hour. I minded my business and she minded hers. I caught her face in the rearview mirror and could tell she'd been crying. Her nose was red and her eyes swollen and glassy. I sat there that first thirty minutes wanting to ask if everything was okay, was there anything I could do to help. Finally, I did.

"Are you okay?"

I half expected her to pull over and kick me out of the car, like who the hell did I think I was. But that's not what she did. Matter of fact, she took full advantage of me asking. After a brief crying spell, she unloaded on me, turning that car into a mobile confessional booth.

"I had an abortion. I don't even know why. I would have been a good mother. A *real* good mother!"

I didn't know what to say so I told her "I'm sorry." I'm not sure why I said it or what it meant. It didn't seem appropriate, yet it did.

She cried harder and I got nervous that she'd crash the car, send us into the median or off into the trees. She couldn't have seen the road too well. Her hair stuck to her face in thin strands, wet with tears, her eyes engorged with the kind of pain that makes you want to flip a car on purpose anyway, never mind that her vision was blocked by a wall of trembling water.

"I could feel her...it. There was a bump in my belly." The woman caressed her stomach gently while she said it. Then she screamed like she was on fire, gripped her blouse and pulled. One of the buttons on her blouse popped off and landed on the dashboard. It was a decoration now, a reminder. I didn't like it sitting there, rocking against the car's speeding tires, forcing me to watch it. The bastard was hypnotizing and I hated everything in the world at that moment.

"Let's talk about forgiveness," she said. "Let's talk about forgiving ourselves."

"Okay."

There was silence for a while, then she wiped her eyes. She could see the road now.

"How do *you* forgive yourself?"

I thought about it and realized I didn't hold regret, not the kind she was talking about. So I pretended I did and told her about the time I slapped that kid, sent him flying off his chair. There were more fights at Gramm Jones, but I told her about that one because it was a slap and not a punch. You get slapped and it's this whole embarrassing thing, like spitting in someone's face or pissing on their back. It's degrading and I know it bruised that kid's ego. All to hell.

When I finished my story she laughed and told me I should forgive myself, that maybe it was the old me. But she was wrong. It wasn't the old me. That slap was still in me. I could feel it winding up every time someone stared too long or asked me what the hell.

I asked her if she felt like the abortion was the old her.

"Hell yes it was. I was sixteen."

The woman couldn't have been younger than 30. She'd been carrying that a long time. Too long.

"You've never told anyone, have you?"

She nodded, and I could see the water walls building again, the button rocked on the dash, and I sat ready to dive into the front seat with my hand on the wheel if needed.

"You can't carry that shit around with you, lady. You need to forget it and move on. I can see your remorse, and I know that baby can, too."

I reached up and swiped the button off the dash, cracked my window and flicked that bitch outside. "That's your past, leave it back there."

We rode for another half hour or so then got off the highway and pulled into a gas station. The woman said that was as far as she was going, then she gave me five bucks for something to eat and drink.

I thanked her and started to get out of the car when she grabbed my arm.

"Wait. I can't ever put a button back on here, can I?" She tugged at her shirt.

I told her no, she can't.

10 - Like a Boy

I bought a sandwich and a small bag of chips. I got a cup of water to save money, but the cashier made me pay him a nickel anyway, said that cups aren't free. I should have stuck my head in a bathroom sink. Every penny counts when you've got no home.

I sat in the parking lot of this gas station, eating my sandwich and drinking my water, and decided to write. I laid a napkin out on a parking block and wrote about the woman and the abortion she wishes she never had. I hoped she moves on. Nobody should carry guilt around for that long. Life doesn't wait for you to forget about things. It just keeps on moving.

A car pulled up near the curb. It was a man and a woman. They were fighting about her hair and how he hated it since she'd gotten it cut. The man told her she looked like a boy now. When they got out of the car I glanced at her. She did look like a boy. Still, you don't pull that shit on your woman. Dick move.

11 - The Suburbs

Back at the gas station, I found out I was in Fort Collins, Colorado. About forty minutes south of Wyoming. No idea how I didn't notice we weren't headed west, that the mountains never got any closer. That woman drove straight north.

After I ate the sandwich I left the gas station. I wanted to head south, maybe even walk all the way back to Denver and start again toward Hermosa, but it'd feel like failure. I was done with Denver. Instead, I stuck around Fort Collins for the day, found myself in a nice little suburb, something I'd never seen outside a movie. Ranch-style homes with carefully trimmed bushes, sprinklers feeding lush, well-kept lawns. It was charming, and I wondered how many of the residents took it for granted.

I wandered the streets for a while, took my time, admired each house. Every one of them had their lawns edged in paver stone, various foliage filling the space across thick layers of mulch or stones. Real prideful work.

I sat on the curb and a cat walked up to me. It was black and white with bright green eyes and a silver collar. Until then, I'd only ever pet a cat once. Sister Jude brought one into Gramm Jones. A kitten. It took right to me, curled up on my lap and purred. But we were supposed to be taking turns, so I had to pass it to the kid next to me, let him pet it. The kitten didn't lie down on his lap like it did mine, so the kid got pissed and tried shoving it off him. The kitten held on to his leg, dug its claws right in there. That kid howled like he was being skinned alive. That's what you get, I guess.

The black and white cat brushed up against my leg and meowed, but its voice was shot, like it'd been smoking its whole life. It rolled in the street on its back and stretched out its legs, clawing at the air. I pulled out a napkin and wrote about the cat. I named him Peter.

12 - Badass and Brand New

I walked the neighborhood some more and saw a garage sale at a small, Spanish style home. The yard was filled with blankets and bedsheets spread out with not much on them—old tools, some clothes, a few puzzles, dishes, and a box of books. That was it. A skinny old man with an old man hat sat in a lawn chair overseeing it all, a TV tray next to him holding a glass of iced tea and a cigar box.

I checked out the books, saw a paperback copy of *I Am Legend* by Richard Matheson. I was familiar with it, saw both film adaptations. Vincent Price did it better. I wanted the book and debated on spending the dime. I didn't want my backpack filling up, but I knew a time would come when I'd wish I had another book on me. I can only read *The Painted Bird* so many times.

On one of the bedsheets, next to a pile of clothes, was a wallet. It was purple with silver lining. Badass and brand new.

"How much for the wallet?"

"A buck." The man never looked at me, stared straight ahead like he was blind. But he wasn't.

When I made it to California I'd get myself a job, would need a wallet to hold my money. And to hold a library card. Whatever Hermosa Beach had in the way of a library, I'd be there often. Still, a dollar was steep.

I opened the wallet. The Velcro was new and ripped loud. I wondered if it'd been opened before. I don't think it had. I stuck my fingers in the little pockets, felt around. I pictured the wallet bulging with bills, a library card in the small pocket with the angled lip for easy access. I pictured a driver's license in there, too. I wasn't gonna hoof it my whole life. Hell no.

"Take fifty cents?"

"Nope."

I set the wallet back on the bedsheet. Had to be wise with my money. If I spent a dollar, I'd have less than two left. Not good. I wasn't hungry now but I would be later. I looked at the wallet again. Bad. Ass. Then walked away to break the seduction.

"I'll tell you what," the old man said, still not looking at me. "You help me bring the rest of the stuff out," nodding toward the house, "and I'll knock a dime off the wallet, give you a glass of tea, too."

The dime didn't mean a thing. I knew I'd still need to save my money, but I figured I'd help the guy, get a beverage out of it. Do a good deed.

The old man pointed me toward a sliding glass door and said to bring out the dining room table and chairs as well as the TV and the end tables. I walked inside. It was a nice house and smelled good, too. The man had a thing for wicker. There were wicker baskets and wicker trays hanging on the wall in the kitchen and above the threshold into the living room and sitting on small shelves along the walls. Some with plants in them, some without. Wicker baskets held the TV and VCR remotes and bananas and apples and utility bills and pens and pencils, all strategically placed through the rooms. There was even a big wicker chair with a giant back like some kind of brittle throne stuffed in the corner. But it all worked somehow.

I took the dining room chairs out and put them where he asked, next to the tools, then went back for the end tables. They were heavy and full of catalogs and TV guides, so I emptied them out, set the end tables out near the road.

The TV was a floor model. A real beauty. It looked like a screen grew right out of a tree. No way I could lift it myself, not even drag it out.

"I'm gonna need your help with the TV," I told the man.

"No can do. Got no legs."

I walked back out of the house, looked at the man, looked at his legs. They were bent at the knee with his feet on the ground, covered in yellow pants. The kind you'd see on a golf course.

"You mean you've got prosthetics or something?"

"No, I mean I ain't got no legs at all."

I looked at his legs again, waited for him to look at me. To see me looking at them. He stared straight ahead.

"If I tell you I ain't got 'em, then they ain't really there, are they?"

His anti-logic made me thirsty. I asked him about the tea.

"Get it yourself. It's in the fridge, sugar on the counter."

I headed back inside.

"Not until you're done," he said.

I grabbed the dining room table, had to turn it on its side and kinda drag it through the slider but I got it, unscathed even, then dragged it over by the chairs and the tools.

"I can't get the TV," I told him.

"Fair enough. Unhook the VCR. I'm thinkin' a hundred bucks. And don't forget the remote."

I got the VCR and the remote.

"There's some tape I left on the kitchen counter next to a marker. Bring that out here and we'll price this junk."

Most of the stuff he priced higher than I would have, except for the VCR. It looked new.

"You may as well help yourself to a sandwich with the tea. And fill mine up, will ya?"

I went inside and topped his glass, then poured my own. I'm not a tea drinker but it hit the spot. I put eight spoonfuls of sugar in mine. I wasn't hungry but I made a sandwich, ham with cheese. I'd save it for later.

Next to the old man was a lawn chair that wasn't there minutes ago. I sat down, gave the guy his tea and stuck the sandwich in the front pocket of my backpack.

"So what happened to your legs?" I gotta tell you. I was real curious, but he avoided the question.

"I can smell your tea from here. You got a sweet tooth."

We watched a few cars go by. They drove slow, checking out what we had to offer. It was nice sitting there with that old man, even if he wouldn't give me the courtesy of glancing my way. Just as well, I guess.

"So ninety cents on the wallet?" I asked.

"I'm feeling like a good guy...fifty."

"Sold." I dug out fifty cents, handed it off, and grabbed my new wallet. Pulled the Velcro apart. Still brand new. Still badass.

"My name's Levi."

"They call me Marz...with a Z."

"Nice to meet you, Marz." I didn't try to shake his hand. I could tell that wasn't his thing.

We talked a little, mostly about how VCRs are changing the world and what comes next. A handful of people showed up, bought some clothes, some tools. Marz told a couple of guys in a pickup there was a TV inside. They carried it out, gave him almost $400 for it. He gave me $10.

"Are you moving?" I asked.

He said he wasn't. I pried a little more, asked him why he was selling everything.

"Boredom."

Then Marz looked right at me and said: "You seem like a good kid. Run."

I was confused, had no idea what he meant. Then he said: "This ain't my house...it's theirs."

And pointed at a station wagon packed with a family, hauling ass toward the house.

"Run!" he yelled.

I grabbed my backpack and hopped the little stucco wall that surrounded the backyard, then over the wall again and into the neighbor's yard. I could hear yelling behind me: "What in the hell!? Who the hell are you!?"

"Don't you yell at a helpless old man! I don't know where I am...I'm crippled!" Then I could hear Marz screaming for help. The guy knew how to play the victim.

No idea how many different lawns I ran through, over fences, through hedgerows. It's like my eyes and ears were still back at the house. Out of body. The next thing I know I'm out of the suburbs and can see the gas station ahead.

I felt a little bad that I'd just helped rob a family—in the most peculiar way I could think of. But, no way in hell I was going back there.

I sat in a patch of grass outside the gas station and put the ten in my badass wallet.

13 - Hell No

For obvious reasons, I didn't stick around Fort Collins. I hitched a ride heading south along I-25 but stopped in Broomfield, just before Denver. The ride was uneventful. I wrote, using my copy of *I Am Legend* as a surface. I'd need more napkins soon.

The gracious soul that picked me up was a middle-aged man in a business suit who listened to gospel music on low. He'd mumble the words like he knew them, but he didn't. Except anytime the word "Jesus" was sung, he'd say that loud and clear. He knew that word.

The guy was going further south but he dropped me off before Denver. I told him I needed to start heading west. He told me that if I was going west—right through the mountains—that it'd be a whole lot easier if I just went through Denver first. I told him hell no.

I spent the rest of the day walking toward the mountains. And then I hit Boulder.

14 - If You Want To

It was dark and I was dead-to-the-world tired, like I wanted to hop in a dumpster, use pizza dough as a pillow. I did end up hitting a dumpster. I was hungry. I'd downed the ham sandwich earlier and was trying to stretch the money.

The dumpster was behind a Chinese restaurant. I struck gold with two containers of rice. One had green beans or some shit mixed with steak. The other was plain. Found a fortune cookie in there too. The fortune said: *You'll go far. If you want to.*

After filling up on dumpster food from the Orient, I headed to a golf course I'd passed on the way. I wasn't sure how early people got up to hit the course but figured crashing clear in the back would keep me from getting caught too early. It ain't fun waking up to a looming face.

This ain't no Holiday Inn.

I slept in a huddle of bushes like before but without the sound of highway wheels lulling me to sleep. Too bad. Instead, the occasional dog barked from a nearby subdivision while the light from a swimming pool cast that white blue I learned to love.

I thought about being less than an hour from Denver after a day of travel. Embarrassing. Tomorrow I'd make my way through the mountains, maybe treat myself to a decent breakfast. Something that didn't come from a gas station or a dumpster.

    Good night, swimming-pool moon.

15 - Her Biggest Fear

I was up before the golfers were out. I lay there for another half hour before I saw any. I watched them play through, chasing their little white balls around. Part of me thought it looked silly—grown men hitting a ball from place to place, dressed in loud clothes and metal cleats. The other part of me wanted to join them.

I wrote a little, then left to find a diner. I was hoping to find something like in the movies, where the waitress—the one with a latchkey kid waiting at home—calls you hon' and wears too much blush and smells of cigarette breaks and last night's gin, but I couldn't find anything like that so I settled for McDonald's. They had a breakfast deal going on—sausage McMuffin, hashbrown, and a medium coffee for a buck twenty-five.

The woman at the counter didn't call me hon', but she did call me sir. It didn't feel right and made me think of Sister Jude and how she used to tell me to never think I don't deserve nice things, a good life, and people's respect. She said her biggest fear for me was that I'd never realize how special I was. She said that lack of self worth kills potential and it kills opportunity. So far her fear had come true.

Before I left McDonald's, I asked for more napkins.

16 - Spray Paint the Walls

I broke down and bought a map. It took some getting used to, using the map. I'd never actually looked at one before. After I figured out exactly where I was, I headed southwest through Boulder on foot. My plan was to reach the outskirts and hit the highway, head south to Golden, and straight west from there. The mountains were getting closer—no longer a hazy beast looming over the horizon. There was definition and color to them. They were gorgeous.

I spent the rest of the morning walking through Boulder. It's a big, beautiful city. I suppose Denver is too, but it's hard to detach my experience in Gramm Jones enough to appreciate it.

I stopped behind a strip mall to take a piss. There was graffiti on the wall—a large, blocky word that was too hard to read. Written over it—in bright red letters—someone had sprayed "Sam was here" with an exclamation point that had a heart at the bottom. I emptied out underneath it, adding my own dot.

Before I was finished, someone opened the backdoor to one of the shops. I think it was a candle store because that's all I could smell—scented wax—and a sticker on the door read *Wicks N' Sticks*. I grabbed my junk and pinched it, cutting off the flow. Hurt like hell. Then I turned away from the door and flipped my stuff back in my pants.

"Don't be messin' around back here, painting these walls. Next time I'll call the police." A man with a white T-shirt, tight jeans, and feathered blonde hair stood propping the door open, letting the scent of candles escape.

"No problem, sir. I wasn't painting anything," I said, as drops of urine soaked into my underwear, turning cold against my skin.

The man kicked a piece of wood underneath the door to keep it open. He just stood there. I was mostly empty. I'd hold the rest until I hit a restroom. It was a stupid move to piss out under the sun like that.

***

I popped into a gas station and grabbed a sandwich, bag of chips, and a Mountain Dew for later. A wise purchase? Probably not. But I was nearing the edge of Boulder. The next meal could be a while. My legs aching from the trek was something I could handle. Going hungry wasn't.

I hit 93 and made my way south, thumb in the wind.

17 - Just a Jog

The road stretched out through grassy lands, the mountains on my right. I watched them as I walked. They never seemed to get closer. These weren't the snow-capped crags that sat further west. These were hilly and littered with trees that looked like stubble on dimpled chins.

A speeding car approached, cut into the side of the road—barely missing me—then hit the brakes. Pebbles crackled, the tires skidding clumsily in the dirt, leaving a grooved trail behind them. My next ride.

It was an old rusted Impala, dark green. Like an avocado painted October. I jogged toward the passenger side, peeked in. The guy driving gave me a once over, then said "What you waitin' for? Hop in."

I did.

"You're in luck." The man hit the gas, then reached into his shirt pocket and pulled out a joint. I knew exactly what it was. Howard Pawnee snuck one into Gramm Jones once, lit it in our room and somehow managed to poke a small hole in the corner of the window using a screwdriver. He tried blowing the smoke outside but it was windy and downtown Denver wanted nothing to do with Howard and his reefer, so the room filled with burnt leaves and skunk. We both got in trouble for that. Dumbass.

The guy handed me the joint, told me to light it, pointed toward the car's lighter, then turned up the radio. I recognized the song. It was *Bitch* by the Stones. A good one.

"Party every day, right?" The guy pointed at my shirt.

He'd really set the tone for a party, alright—the tunes, a ride on a stretch of country road under a blue sky, Jagger singing about how love's a bitch. But I wasn't interested.

"No thanks."

He turned *Bitch* down, looked at me.

"Well, Sheeeeeiiiit."

The car filled with whatever alcohol clung to his tongue. I started to think taking the ride was a bad idea. Why leave Gramm Jones to go hungry, bust my ass and piss my pants only to wind up with my head through a drunk's windshield?

"This'll do." I pointed to a small house buried in knee-high grass.

"That your house?"

"Yep."

"You a squatter?"

"Nah, meeting some friends." I'm not a good liar, and it was obvious. The guy hit the brakes and slid along the side of the road—an instant replay from when he picked me up.

"The hell you asking for a ride for when you're damn near there? Hitchin' ain't no safe bet. You don't flag down strangers for just a jog down the road, ya know?"

The guy was pissed. I couldn't tell if he was offended by me declining the party or about the short ride. I opened the door and stepped out, before he took off again.

"Your shirt sucks," he said, then floored it, spitting out a cloud of dust that swallowed me.

I knew there'd be all kinds, good and bad—mostly bad—so I didn't let it get to me. When the dust settled, I sat on the side of the road and downed the sandwich, the chips, and the Dew. It hit the spot.

I looked down at my shirt. Most of the glitter was gone now. The guy was right. My shirt sucked.

18 - Boys from Compton

I walked the rest of the way to Golden, got there early evening, exhausted and ready to sleep. There wasn't much around—a new subdivision being built, a 7-Eleven, and a sub shop. Still no diner.

I could tell I was on the outskirts, that there was more to the town than just that lone intersection. I stopped at the sub shop and used the bathroom, then asked for a water. I offered to pay a nickel for it, but they gave it up for free. I sat in the parking lot and watched the people at the 7-Eleven. It wasn't quite dark yet, but they had the overhead fluorescents on. It was like moonlight.

Two young girls—around 16, probably—were standing near the ice machine, talking, when a guy walked up to them, looked them up and down like they were menus. Words were exchanged, but I couldn't tell what, then the guy yelled "Stupid bitches!" and walked away. Another guy hopped out of a car and charged the first guy. When he got to him he didn't punch him or tackle him. He just picked him up off the ground by his shirt and shook him side to side, screaming: "You wanna talk shit, dickhead!? You wanna talk shit!?" The guy's shoes flew off in different directions, and he ended up on the ground, yelling: "My boys from Compton are comin' for you, man! You're dead!" Then he gathered his shoes like they were textbooks in the hall at high school.

I started laughing. I hadn't laughed for a long time.

19 - Three's Company

I sat looking across the street toward the hilly mountain. In less than 10 minutes I could be at the top of it, looking down across the highway, over the parking lots and their moonlight fluorescents. I wondered what could be on the other side of that mountainy hill. More hills? Or larger mountains off in the distance? The white-capped crags. The kind the guy on TV painted with his palette knife, in-between beating the devil out of his brush.

I had decided I'd go ahead and sleep on top of the mountain when I heard glass break. Two women were exiting the 7-Eleven, a jar of pickles smashed at their feet. The women were overweight and heavily encumbered by their own breasts, hidden beneath too many grocery bags. I grabbed my backpack, strapped it on and ran to help.

"Need a hand?" I asked, as I grabbed a bag from each of them.

"Bless your heart. We're going right over here." One of the women nodded toward a Winnebago in the far corner of the parking lot.

The RV had a bumper sticker on the back that said *Will Brake for Love* and another of a tie-dye heart. One of the women set down her groceries and opened the door to the Winnebago while the other woman headed in, dropped the bags on a counter and came back to fetch mine.

"Any relish?" A man's voice from inside the RV.

"No dill, only sweet, so we bought a jar of pickles...but Lori dropped it."

"Sorry, hon'," Lori said.

"It's alright. We'll find some," the man's voice said.

"We got us some help, though. A strong young man by the name of..."

"Levi."

The woman stepped aside and waved me in. I climbed in.

"Hi, I'm Levi." I walked to the front of the RV where a thin man with curly red hair and thick glasses sat behind the steering wheel, reading a map that stretched across the dash and covered the windshield. He turned toward me and extended his hand. We shook. I tried looking in his eyes while he introduced himself but one was slightly off and I couldn't tell which, so I'd alternate—give my attention to one, then the other.

"Nice to meet you, Levi. I'm Scottie. Thanks for helping out."

"Not a problem. Glad I could."

"I'm Hannah." The woman behind me held out her hand. She was a big girl with long brown hair. The kind of hair you see in shampoo commercials. The kind most women dream of having, I suppose.

The RV rocked as Lori took the steps and entered. She wasn't as big as Hannah, but close.

"Hi. I'm Lori...I dropped the pickles." I shook Lori's hand. She had a bandana on her head that was covered in purple and green paisley. No hair leaked out from under, and her eyebrows were gone. She was hairless.

"You from Golden, Levi?" Scottie asked.

"Denver."

"We're from Utah," Hannah said.

"Yep, decided to go on a camping trek. Get away from it all and what not," Scottie said. "What are you doing in Golden?"

"I'm on my way to Hermosa Beach. It's in California."

"Nice. Northern or southern?" Scottie asked.

"Southern."

"Right on. What's out there?"

"My dad."

The words just came out. I don't know why. Maybe there was a little hope there when Sister Jude told me about the surfer with a face like mine, but it was a small hope. One that I tried not to entertain.

Hannah looked me up and down, saw my backpack and said "You're hitchin' it, aren't you?"

I nodded.

"Scottie?" Hannah said.

Scottie looked at each girl, nodded, then looked at me. "Levi, you wanna join us for a few days? We're heading west tomorrow, back to Utah. But it's the best route through the mountains. We got plenty of room for you, both in the tents and here in the Regal Beagle." He slapped the dashboard with his hand when he gave the RV's name.

"You sure?"

"Definitely," Lori said.

"You're more than welcome," Scottie said.

"You sure are," Hannah added.

It seemed like a good idea, so I tagged along.

20 - Buffalo Bill Didn't Hate Indians

I sat up front with Scottie while the girls made sandwiches in the back. I could hear them talking about Lori's bandana and how pretty it was and how much it helped.

We drove through Golden. It's a lot different than Denver. It's small and surrounded tight by mountainous terrain. Claustrophobic and comforting all at once. Scottie pointed out some stores they visited earlier that day, including the one where they'd bought Lori's bandana.

"We gotta show you Lookout Mountain." Scottie said. "You'll love it."

Scottie grabbed a pack of Marlboro 100s off the island between our seats and offered me one. I took the pack. One of the cigarettes was upside down. I didn't grab that one. I pushed in the lighter on the dash and Scottie pulled it right back out.

"We don't use that. Hannah won't allow it. When she was young, the lighter in her daddy's car flew out and under the seat. Caught fire under there and torched the car. Use that lighter."

He nodded to the island. There was a Bic sitting in one of the cup holders. It had a largemouth bass on it, jumping out of the water. It made me want to fish, something I'd never done before, only read about in Field & Stream or saw in movies. I always thought I'd be good at it.

I lit my cigarette and handed the pack and the lighter to Scottie. He took the upside-down cigarette without knowing it, put it in his mouth and lit the filter. It caught on fire and he took a hit that made him cough and curl his lip. But he played it off like nothing was wrong and hit the smoke again. Pride. I could tell he hated every bit of it, smoking that burning filter.

I hit my cigarette. I'd had a few before but never inhaled. This time I did. I was careful, though. I just took a small hit and didn't hold it in. That way I didn't cough.

Scottie's cigarette was starting to reek up the RV. He finally put it out like he just wasn't interested in smoking it either way, and then yelled back at Lori.

"Lori! I told you luck don't come from cigarettes. Will you cut it with that shit, already?"

"Sorry," she said, then giggled. Hannah did too.

"We've got no KISS on the Beagle, but we've got some Alice. Same thing, right?" Scottie said.

He told me to open the glovebox and grab the Alice Cooper cassette. The glove box was filled with tapes, mostly with no cases: Molly Hatchet, 38 Special, Meatloaf, Elton John and Alice Cooper—one of the few that had a case. I took out the tape and handed it to him. He shoved it in the deck and turned up the volume. Hannah and Lori sang all the lyrics together. It wasn't like anything I'd heard Alice sing before. This was tame. A song about a man coming home and worried how his woman is gonna see him now because he always lets her down—a love song with too much piano. Nothing about spiders or dead things or nightmares. I stared at the tape cover and pretended Alice hadn't let me down.

***

It wasn't long before we were at Lookout Mountain. We parked and Scottie ran over to a little fenced area and whipped out, started pissing through the fence.

"Join me, Levi!" Scottie yelled.

I walked over to the fence. It was a small wrought-iron enclosure protecting a stone monument inside. There was a plaque on it, but I didn't read it.

"Let loose on the grave, man. It's Buffalo Bill's."

"You're pissing on it?" I asked.

"'Yep. He hated the Indians."

"No he didn't," I argued.

"That's what my old man told me. He stood right here on this spot and told me. We pissed on it together." Scottie zipped up.

I wasn't gonna argue with him. I was a guest.

"You'd better not be spreadin' hate to that boy, Scottie." Hannah yelled from the RV. Her and Lori both had their arms full of blankets and pillows.

I followed the girls through the parking area and into the grass. They told me not to look and one of them held my hand, guiding me. I stared at the ground, being careful not to stumble and let them lead me. I trusted them.

"Don't peek." Hanna kept saying.

I heard other voices and smelled weed and cigarettes. The ground under me went from flat to sloping as we started downhill. Then they both told me to stop and look.

We stood at the top of a grassy mountain, up 7,500 feet over the city below, our view stretching for miles.

"Golden looks enormous from up here," I said.

"Honey, only part of that is Golden. The rest is Denver," Lori said.

Denver. I couldn't seem to get away from it. But when towering over it like that I felt victorious, the view below nonthreatening. Every star had dropped from the sky and found a new home on earth—an orgy of lights completely man made yet otherworldly in appearance. A celestial paradise of varying colors. I wondered which one of those lights was Gramm Jones and felt bad for the kids inside—the same walls, the same views––while I stood free, staring straight into Heaven.

I sat on the grass and pulled some napkins from my backpack and wrote my thoughts. Even if I did have a camera it would never do it justice. My words would paint the picture.

Lori and Hannah spread out two blankets on the ground while Scottie hit a joint shared by a nearby couple. Spread across the mountain top were more blankets with small groups of people, mostly couples making out or holding hands, unable to fight the romanticism of the sight before them. If I had a girlfriend, I imagine we'd be up here too.

Hannah walked over to partake with Scottie and his new friends, and Lori patted the space next to her, inviting me to sit.

"It's beautiful, isn't it?"

"It really is." I said.

We sat silent for a while, gazing and listening to the murmur of couples.

"I feel less alone whenever we come up here, like closer to the universe or something," Lori said.

"Levi!" Scottie yelled for me, held up the joint. I shook my head no and he turned back to his new friends, taking another hit.

"Why do you feel alone? You've got Hannah and Scottie," I said.

Lori picked at fuzz on the blanket.

"Yeah, I do. But things are different than they used to be."

I could tell she wanted to open up about stuff, but I didn't want to hear it. I had my own shit going on, and I never considered myself any good at providing a sturdy shoulder, especially to strangers. But I gave in. I bit.

"How so?"

"Scottie spends more time with Hannah now. It used to be equal. We've just always had this unspoken agreement that we share Scottie equally. But I think the only reason he sleeps with me anymore is out of pity. He feels bad, because..."

She stopped picking fuzz and looked out over Denver. The reflection in her eyes grew larger as tears pooled on her lids.

"Because I have breast cancer."

The tears spilled over. Scottie's stoned laughter nearby was a knife in my ears.

"I'm in remission, but they told me I should get them removed."

"Your breasts?" I asked.

Lori nodded. "What's a woman without her tits?"

I looked at Lori's chest. Her breasts were large and looked uncomfortable resting on her plump stomach. I pictured her without them and wondered if she wouldn't be happier losing the encumbrance. But then I thought of my own parts and decided even if my pecker hindered my walk and my balls too big to wear jeans, I'd still want them.

"There's a lot more to a woman than just her breasts," I said. "A whole lot more. And if it means saving your life, then you shouldn't hesitate leaving them behind. You're a good person, Lori...Tits or no tits."

She grabbed my hand and held it.

"That's sweet of you, Levi. Thank you. Can I ask you a question?"

"Sure."

"Do you feel alone sometimes? Because of...your face?"

A kick to the gut. I should have seen it coming, but I didn't. I think it's because for a moment I forgot who I was.

"Quite a bit."

"You're unique, Levi."

"I guess that's one way of looking at it."

"Maybe when you reach your dad you'll feel less lonely."

My dad.

"Yeah, maybe."

Lori and I held hands, and I watched Scottie and Hannah and wondered if I wasn't there would Lori be sitting alone.

The four of us spent the rest of the evening on the blankets, talking. Lori got a headache so Hannah took off Lori's bandana and massaged her bald head and rubbed at her temples. Scottie wouldn't look at Lori while her bandana was off. He seemed disgusted. The girls told me all about Utah and how they met Scottie. The two girls were roommates and worked at the same diner, when Scottie showed up one day looking for a meal and a place to live. They felt bad and took him in. His charisma did the rest, they said. I told them I'd always wanted to eat at a homestyle diner. They said maybe we'd find one on the way.

Before we left, I mustered up as much phlegm as my body would allow and spit it all toward Gramm Jones and toward every shallow asshole. The spit did nothing but fall from my mouth and drop to the grass. If I could piss with the pressure of a geyser, I'd do that too. Toward them all. Instead, I gave beautiful Denver the finger and headed back to the Regal Beagle.

21 - Blueberry Toast

We'd spent the night in a park near Lookout Mountain and woke up early. I slept in a small pup tent while Lori slept in the Beagle and Hannah and Scottie in a larger tent. I'm not sure how things usually were with their triangle—if they normally all slept together or took turns or what—but I felt bad for Lori. She deserved a man to herself and could do better than Scottie. The guy was clueless. Or he just didn't give a shit.

Scottie had built a fire before the rest of us got up. I got out of my tent and sat near him on the ground. We talked about the smell of Colorado mornings and how coffee sounded good. He told me to get the pie irons from the Beagle. I told him I didn't know what that was, and he said Lori would show me, to just knock and head on in.

I knocked and Lori answered the door, let me in. She'd been up putting makeup on. Her penciled eyebrows didn't look good, but she tried. She tried for Scottie. And that asshole didn't know he had a good one with her.

Lori gave me the pie irons—two long poles with cast iron plates that hooked together at the end. I took them to Scottie and he showed me how they worked. He put a slice of bread in each plate, then poured in blueberry filling from a can and clamped it together and held it over the fire. It flattened, sealed, and toasted the bread. Then we dipped the blueberry pies in syrup, like it made it feel more like breakfast with syrup involved. But really it was just bread and pie filling and altogether too sweet.

Hannah came out from a group of trees with arms full of sticks for the fire. Her usually flowing hair was matted to her face with sweat and bits of grass.

"Put them here," Scottie said, and pointed to the ground next to him.

Hannah and Lori brought chairs from the RV and set them around the fire for us. I offered to help but Scottie grabbed my arm and said they'd do it, that they liked to serve.

Once everyone had a chair and had eaten their blueberry pie, Scottie had us all join hands while he said a prayer of sorts:

"We give our day to you, Father Earth. And we thank you for the sticks for our fire and for the pies. They were damn good. We ask that you bring back Lori's beauty and save the tits. And we'd like to thank you for the bandana you provided to hide the mess in the meantime."

I opened my eyes and looked at Lori. Her eyes were shut painfully tight, her chin quivered. I looked at Hannah. She glared angrily at Scottie who held his face to the sky, his eyes closed. Hannah's nostrils flared, her knuckles white and shaking as she gripped Lori's hand.

"To you our day is given, Father Earth. Amen," Scottie finished.

"Amen," the girls mumbled.

"Today we head through the mountains and hit Utah," Scottie said, then looked at me. "Still coming?"

Without a doubt.

22 - Too Close to See

Most of US-6 followed alongside a rock-filled creek. Driving through the mountains was like rushing through the earth's veins. As we wound along curvy blacktop, the scene ahead was blocked by more mountains, towering crags on either side of us. At one point we stopped on a wide shoulder and drank from the creek. The water was cool and refreshing, the best I'd ever had. But as I bent down, I could hear Scottie laugh while I struggled to sip the water.

"You're an ass," I could hear Hannah say under her breath.

I ignored Scottie and watched the creek break around the jutting rocks, the sound of racing water peaceful and mesmerizing.

"What's say we hike up that incline over there and have us a sandwich?"

None of us seemed to be in the mood but nobody said otherwise. Instead, Lori said, "I'll make some," and headed back to the Beagle. Hannah followed.

"Ever seen anything like this, Levi?" He spread his arms out and slowly spun around.

"Sure haven't."

The scenery was incredible, but I kept thinking of the girls. I wanted to help them. I was tired of seeing them wait on Scottie.

Scottie lit a smoke and asked if I wanted one. I passed. I told him I was going to get my backpack, then headed to the Beagle. I looked at the sticker on the back of the RV that said *Will Brake for Love* and wondered if either of those poor girls knew what love was, because they sure as hell weren't getting it from Scottie. I imagined they were desperate for what they thought a man could offer them, someone to take their mind off their shit life at the diner and their shit apartment. Someone to make them feel like a woman. The problem was, they weren't getting any of that. I could tell, but they couldn't. They were standing too close to see.

I did what I could to help with the sandwiches, then helped carry them back to Scottie, who was drawing in the dirt with a stick. We walked on the side of the rocky incline through brittle grass the color of dirt. At the top was a rocky ledge that overlooked the road, thirty feet below.

We sat on the dirt near the ledge and ate the sandwiches and drank from a canteen Scottie had filled with creek water. He said another prayer to Father Earth, giving thanks, and asking for a shower soon so Hannah could get herself clean and presentable. After the girls gave their hesitant amens, I spoke up and asked Scottie what the hell.

"I think you're a chauvinist, man."

Scottie just kind of stared at me, like he was trying to figure out if he heard me right. The girls, their mouths dropped for sure.

"You treat these ladies like shit while you sit on your ass and order them around. I'll bet that's not even your RV. I'll bet it's theirs, along with everything in it."

Lori started gathering things and nervously talking about how we should get out of the sun and back on the road because we're making good time. Hannah just stared, shocked.

"Listen here, freak. You don't come into what's mine, talkin' shit you know nothing about."

"They're not yours."

"The hell they aren't. Boy, you just lost your ride. Let's go, girls. This kid's overstayed his welcome."

"We can't leave Levi out here in the middle of nowhere," Hannah said.

"The hell we can't. And we will. Now let's go!"

The girls sat, unmoving.

"They're not yours," I reminded him.

"Speak again and I'll beat the hell out of that ugly face of yours."

"Scottie, leave him alone," Hannah said.

Lori began to cry.

"I said let's go!" Scottie grabbed Hannah by the hand and pulled hard, harder than he needed to. But she pulled back and his grip slipped, sending him over the ledge, bouncing off the rocky slope as he fell to the ground, the smack of bone breaking and flesh splitting with each knock against the cliff.

The two girls screamed and peered over the ledge. Scottie lay in the dirt, one of his arms hidden under his body, jagged ivory wrapped in muscle poked out from his shoulder, his face a mask of blood and Colorado earth.

The girls both ran down the incline, Lori skidding on her thigh halfway down. I followed. As we approached Scottie, he made no sound, except for the small red bubble that popped from one nostril, letting us know he was still breathing.

The girls were terrified. I was too. Scottie may have been an asshole but he didn't deserve that. To get beaten by Father Earth.

"What do we do? Do we carry him to the Beagle?" Hannah asked.

"No, we shouldn't move him. We could make things worse." Lori said.

"Then what in the hell do we do?"

"I don't know, Hannah. Maybe one of us could take the Beagle and go get help."

"I don't even know how far it is to the next town, do you?" Hannah asked.

"I think we should carry him." I said. "By the time we get help, they'll still have to drive all the way here. He could die by then. There's a lot of blood."

"You're right." Lori said. "I'll get his legs, you guys grab his..."

We all looked at the broken arm buried beneath his body, like it was something we shouldn't touch—a turd on a restroom floor.

"Hannah, you grab that shoulder. I'll get this side," I said, nodding to the butchered mess where his collarbone poked through. Or maybe it was a splintered shoulder blade.

We picked him up. It was hard to do without sinking my thumb through the wound. I grabbed Scottie's arm and rested it on his chest. I could hear bone against bone, like gritting sand between your teeth.

Lori was crying and Hannah hyperventilating. I told them not to look at him but to look at the ground and watch their step. We passed by the spot where Scottie had drawn in the dirt. Carved into the ground were four stick figures—one was well-rounded with long flowing hair, another was bald with X's for breasts, one with a skull face, and the fourth with curly hair and a halo above its head. We all saw the figures but pretended we didn't.

Once we got to the Beagle we set Scottie in the dirt to open the door, then talked about the best way to carry him up the steps. I looked at him. He didn't look good, but he was still breathing.

Once inside, we set him on one of the beds, and Lori did her best to create a tourniquet above his shoulder using an old sheer curtain. They wanted me to drive so they could stay with him. I'd never driven before. Right of way, merging, and 4-way stops I wasn't sure on, but I could step on pedals and tap a blinker. Hell, you can learn that from any action movie.

I started the RV, put it in drive, and rolled out from the shoulder. The size of the Beagle was intimidating. This was no souped up sports car, low to the ground, handling curves with tight precision. This was a boat on land—awkward and in the way.

I could hear the girls in the back, begging Scottie to be okay and praying for a miracle, praying to God. I wondered what Scottie would think of that.

I told the girls that one of them should check the map. None of us knew where the hell we were. I thought we should go back the way we came. We'd left Golden less than an hour before our stop. But Hannah screamed at me to move ahead on US-6. Ten minutes later she told me to stop and turn around. She'd found our place on the map, and going back was the closest way to help.

I drove until I found another wide shoulder, then turned around. In between winding curves, I broke the speed limit. It was freeing. I rolled down the window and ignored the panic in the back, focused on the road. My hands gripped tight to the steering wheel while 38 Special sang about holding on loosely.

It felt like a moment I've waited my whole life for—the speeding road under my feet, the wind against my face, and air that didn't smell of Colfax and forgotten children. Except there was a broken man in back.

We pulled out of the mountains and around the last curve. The road went from two lanes to five, then seven as we neared an intersection. I didn't know what the hell. A green sign was stuck in the ground with two words I didn't care to see, one in particular: *Denver. Boulder.* Each word had its own white arrow pointing in opposite directions.

"Which way? Straight?"

"Yes," Lori said.

"I can't tell where a hospital is on this thing. Stop at the first place you see that might have a phone," Hannah said.

When approaching the intersection, I stayed out of any lane with an arrow pointing anywhere but straight. The light was yellow. I kept going. Half a mile up the road I turned right, then into the parking lot of a strip mall that was home to a Mexican restaurant and a video store. The video store had a giant poster in the window for the movie Day of the Dead, appropriate somehow.

Hannah ran screaming from the Beagle and into the video store. Lori asked me if I thought Scottie would be okay. I got up and looked at him. His face was streaked red. The bleeding from his arm looked like it was under control and had hardened to a pudding-like plug, holding the rest of his life inside.

"I don't know. I hope so."

"Even though he said those awful things? Even though he doesn't treat us right?"

I nodded yes and wondered if *she* wanted him to live. I looked through the windshield and thought I could see Hannah on the phone. I felt bad. All I really wanted to do was forget about Scottie and the Beagle and the weird love triangle and go in the store and look at the movies on the wall. Just something else on a very long list of simple things I'd never done.

Scottie moaned.

"Levi! He's waking up!"

Scottie opened his eyes enough for the light to reflect off them, then tried to sit up.

"No, honey. You need to lie down, you've been hurt."

"I need a smoke." Scottie said. His voice sounded funny, like he had a cold. Or a nose full of pudding.

I fetched a pack of cigarettes off the island and the lighter.

"Not those. I need a lucky cigarette."

Lori opened her purse and grabbed her pack. There were still four in it—one of them upside down.

"There's still more left in the pack, Scottie. It won't be lucky," Lori said.

"How many are left?" Scottie asked, grunting.

"Four."

"Everybody smoke up...smoke 'em for me. I need the luck...bad."

Lori lit herself a cigarette then handed me one. I didn't want it but took it anyway.

"Where's Hannah?" Scottie asked.

"She's getting help," Lori said.

"I'll wait."

Scottie stared at the bunk above him, his teeth clenched tight. He rolled his eyes a few times. I thought he may pass out. Finally, the Beagle rocked to one side. Hannah had come back.

"Take the cigarette, Hannah," Scottie moaned.

"Scottie!" Hannah knelt beside him.

Lori handed her a cigarette, lit it. All three of us smoked like it was some ceremony—the summoning of luck for the belittling chauvinist. Lori took out the lucky cigarette, put it in Scottie's mouth and lit it. He puffed at it like it'd been days since he'd had one. He went to take it out of his mouth using his broken arm. I could tell because I saw muscles move and heard a wet sound like a ball dropped in mud. He didn't know about his arm yet. He looked over at his shoulder, then sprayed vomit above his head against the bottom bunk, where it stuck temporarily and rained down in drips, burning his eyes.

Then he passed out.

23 - Will Break for Love

The ambulance showed up and took Scottie away. Hannah rode with him while Lori took the Beagle and followed behind. They both hugged me and cried a little when I said I was moving on. I told them they were beautiful women who have something really special to offer and not to let anyone make them feel like they don't deserve the best. They knew I was talking about Scottie.

"I hope you find a home-style diner, Levi," Lori said, then she pulled out to follow the ambulance.

I watched the Beagle pull away and read the bumper sticker one last time and thought about how Scottie *did* break for love, just not how he would have wanted.

24 - The Masked Ones

Three days had passed since I left Gramm Jones, yet I was less than an hour away. I should have been out of Colorado altogether.

I hit the dumpster behind the Mexican restaurant, but it was a mess and I still had $8.40 left. I spent a good half hour in the video store, looking at the tape covers on the wall and along the aisles, all marked by genre. It sounds cliché, but I really did feel like a kid in a candy store. Except the candy was off limits without a VCR and a couch to sit on. I wondered if Hermosa Beach had a video store like this one. After lots of hard work, maybe I could get myself a VCR and rent movies. Movies and books. I pictured a house—my house—packed with shelves containing both. My own libraries where I'd take my time choosing which world I'd escape to.

One of the store employees followed me around, asking me questions about horror films. He showed a real passion for the genre, and seemed interested in my opinion on his favorites, like *Friday the 13th* and *Halloween* and *The Texas Chainsaw Massacre*.

Then he asked me if I'd seen the movie *Mask*, and I knew what the hell. So I got out of there and headed south on the outskirts of Golden. I decided to take a different route. I didn't want to see US-6 again, especially the spot where Scottie fell, and the figures of us he drew on the ground.

Before hitting I-70, I stopped at a gas station and bought a hot dog, a pickle, and a V8. The V8 gave me a craving for cheese, and I wrote about it and about Scottie and the girls while I sat outside the gas station. Then I numbered the napkin pages and stacked them in order. I'd need more napkins soon, and maybe another pen.

25 - Snuff Changes You

While walking along I-70, I wondered if Gramm Jones had reported me missing or if they just wrote me off, with some swaying from Sister Jude. She'd know I was safe, that I was just doing what I needed to do. She might have even known where I was headed. I'd send her a postcard one day and thank her, let her know I really was okay.

***

About a half an hour onto I-70, I got a ride from a man in a pickup who said he was heading to Vail, about ninety minutes up the road. He told me if I liked to ski then I'd love Vail, that maybe I could even get a job there because they're always hiring young people. I thanked him for the info and changed the subject. I was California bound. Colorado could kiss my ass.

The guy's name was Randy. We talked about movies the whole time. He liked westerns. He said he had a whole VHS collection full of them at home. I wasn't real familiar with westerns, they were never my thing, but I liked hearing Randy talk about them because he was really passionate about it, like they really did it for him. It's nice to hear someone go on about something they're passionate about, no matter what it is.

That passion is contagious. Hell, by the time we got to Vail I wanted to catch a western myself.

He talked about spaghetti westerns mostly. He said since I like horror movies that maybe I'd like those because some were gory, especially the Peckinpah films. I'd heard of Peckinpah.

Turns out we both liked Hitchcock, though he'd seen more of his films than I had. He named some that I'd never even heard of. Then he asked me if I'd ever seen a snuff film.

"You get the chance to, you turn it down, Levi. Never, ever watch that shit. It'll change you. It changed me."

"How?" I asked.

"I don't sleep like I used to. I used to sleep on my back, my arms by my side. But I can't anymore. Makes me feel like I'm in a coffin, like I'm dead."

"What'd you see?"

"I saw a man die, Levi. Right on tape!"

I got the impression he wanted to keep talking about it, so I pressed him for details.

"How'd he die?"

"He was electrocuted, execution style, strapped to the chair. He foamed all up. Blood poured from his eyes like you wouldn't believe. It was real."

"Did his eyes pop?" I'd read that's what can happen.

"Maybe. They had tape over them. I'm telling you, boy... you don't want to see none of that snuff shit."

I thought about how I watched Scottie fall, seeing his broken body in the dirt, the sounds it made on the way down, and wondered if that would change me. Like if I started getting recurring nightmares or developed a fear of heights or maybe just started hating the mountains altogether. I decided that I'd fight any change I felt coming. That if I looked at a mountain with fear in my gut, I'd race toward it and climb that bitch to the top.

26 - Hippie Kid & Mr. Toasty

Randy dropped me off in Vail. It's a small village that sits in the middle of the tree-covered mountains and is home to the state's largest ski resort. Walking through Vail, with the mountains in every background and the wood-trimmed buildings, it made me think of Switzerland or Germany.

I walked through the village and found a little store, so I bought some juice. It felt less awkward walking around with something to do with my hands. When I got a strange look I'd focus on my juice, take a gulp.

I ended up on a trail that left the village and went over a wooden bridge. I took a seat on the bank of a small stream, finished my juice, then filled it up with the stream water and stuck it in my backpack for later. The stream was peaceful and I focused on it instead of on Scottie and his fall, which was taking up too much of my time since it happened.

It was my hope that Lori and Hannah would get away from him, leave him alone to piss on graves, hunt for dill relish, and live off blueberry sandwiches. The stream helped to collect my thoughts. I even wrote some more. Then I saw two kids heading down the trail toward me. They looked a few years older than me and I got anxious, stuffed the napkin and the pen in my backpack, zipped it. I get like that when I'm around other kids. I know how cruel they can be.

"Hey, dude. You got a smoke?" One of them asked.

I stood, shook my head no.

"You workin' this year?" the same guy asked. He wore a bandana around his neck with a slew of necklaces on that looked uncomfortable. His jeans were rolled up and he had no shoes on. He thought he was some kind of hippie. The other guy was taller and just stood there like he didn't know what the hell. I could tell he was stoned, maybe too many times.

I remembered what Randy said about Vail hiring young people through the year. I told him no, that I wasn't working.

"Just passing through then?"

"Yeah."

"They're hiring, you know. I could get you in."

It's like Colorado didn't want to let go. I told him thanks but I wasn't sticking around.

"Wanna come up to our tent, smoke a bowl?" The tall kid finally spoke.

"Dude, not everyone wants to smoke."

"Well they should."

The hippie kid rolled his eyes, made sure I saw, like it was an apology on behalf of his burned-out friend. They seemed nice enough so I got conversant before things got awkward.

"You guys work here?"

"In the winter we work the lifts, but right now I'm working at that little shop right there." The hippie kid squinted with one eye and pointed off toward the buildings. "And he works at one of the restaurants, cooking."

"Until they find out I killed a man," the tall kid said.

"Whatever, dude." Hippie kid rolled his eyes again, then leaned in toward me like his friend wouldn't hear and said: "He says he clubbed some dude at Safeway with a bat, self defense."

"I did, man. Blood everywhere. I knew that dude wasn't getting up after that. And he never did. They carried him away on a gurney, the sheet right over his head." He mimed a sheet over his head.

Hippie kid was staring off, shaking his head like he was telling me not to listen because his friend was full of shit.

"Come on, Mister Toasty," the hippie kid said, tugging at his friend's shirt. "We'll see you around, dude. Safe journeys." He threw me a peace sign. His spacey friend touched my shirt as they passed by and said "Kissssss," and then started laughing that quiet, airy laugh that stoners do, like they don't even have the energy to kick one out anymore, like they've exceeded their laugh allotment and it's all they've got now. I could tell hippie kid was different, though. He was on his way out. The stoner thing just wasn't his scene. His friend was a poster child for

everything he didn't want to be. Good for him.
It's the impression I got, anyway.

27 - Britton

Vail was nice, but I didn't want to stick around. Too many people my age. I took to I-70 again, thumb out. Fifteen minutes later I'm riding in the back of an old pickup truck with a golden retriever named Britton. I sat down, my back to the driver, the dog's head on my lap, and just watched the mountains pass by. Britton was about as good as they come and made me want a dog of my own, travel the country by my side. It was selfish thinking. Finding food on the daily just for me was hard enough. A dog like Britton deserved more than dumpster food and gas station heat-lamp leather. Maybe once I got settled in Hermosa.

I wanted to write, but the ride was bumpy. The old truck had traded its shocks for rust. So I spoke to Britton to kill time. I talked about Gramm Jones and Sister Jude and about Scottie and his fall and about what an asshole he was to Lori and Hannah. I told Britton my hopes and dreams—to get a VCR and have my own little library and that I hoped to meet that someone out there who's just like me. It felt good to speak everything out loud. Even if my voice was buried under the sound of 60 miles per hour, Britton was a good listener.

The wind stirred up smells that I think were me. I needed to find a place I could shower, maybe even wash my clothes. I didn't want to give people another reason to turn their heads.

The man drove for what must have been two hours, maybe more, before tapping on the window and asking if I wanted to keep heading west because he was heading south soon. I told him it depends on if we're out of Colorado yet. He kind of chuckled, then said something I couldn't hear. He stopped right before an off ramp and I pet Britton one last time, hopped out, walked up to the driver and told him thanks.

"Thank *you*, young man. Britton's leavin' us today. I appreciate you keeping him company in his last few hours."

"What do you mean?" I asked.

"He's an old boy, gotta put him down. Pissin' and shittin' all through the house, total incontinence. I'm surprised he didn't let go back there."

I felt the back of my jeans. They were wet with urine. I hadn't noticed.

"Plus, he's deaf."

I didn't know what killed me more, confessing on deaf ears—even if they were canine—or that Britton was on his last truck ride ever. I told the driver to wait while I went back and gave Britton one more good pet and wished him well, wherever he was going.

28 - Weight

I needed some reading time. Life was kicking my ass. Real good. This is why we have books and movies, to get away. I wasn't about to read *The Painted Bird* again. If you've read it, you understand. And *I Am Legend* didn't sound appealing either—a man alone in the world, struggling for answers and survival. I guess I needed something with hope. I decided I'd spend the day looking for a used bookstore. I still had six bucks left. I needed to grab a few books. I didn't care how big they were. Nothing could be heavier on my back than the world was right then.

Clifton, Colorado was just ahead. I wrestled with the map and found my way. The map was getting easier to follow. But it was still hard to judge the time of travel. The edge of Utah didn't look too far off. If I had to guess, I'd say no more than three hours by car, maybe only two. The mountains seemed to verify Utah's approach. They were starting to look different. More rocky and layered like stacks of pancakes sliced deep with a fork. I was getting hungry.

29 - A Cherry Sunburst Les Paul

I decided to hit a dumpster instead of buying a meal. I found a McDonald's with a dumpster hidden by bushes. I didn't mind diving in the day if it wasn't out in the open. I've got dignity. But I'm smart, too. Smart enough to know that six bucks doesn't go far. I grabbed a fish sandwich, two hamburgers, and about eight cheeseburgers. All of them wrapped. I ate three of the cheeseburgers, and stuck everything else in my backpack.

Down the road was a guitar store. I stopped in. The walls were lined with guitars of all types. I'm about as good at naming guitars as I am cars. I can't. But I did see one that I knew right away: a cherry sunburst Les Paul. Just like Ace Frehley's. They even had a plaque with his name next to the guitar.

I saw a few people sitting around, plugged in and playing. So when a guy asked me if I needed any help I asked him if I could play the Les Paul. He got it down from the wall and handed it to me, then started plugging it in. I told him not to, that I can't really play, that I just wanted to hold it.

"You want some lessons? We've got a great teacher here."

"Nah. Thanks, though."

While I sat on the top of an amp, the guitar in my lap, I added something else to my growing list of hopes—a guitar, with fingers that knew how to play it. My whole life I wanted to be Ace Frehley, and while I didn't know if this was his actual guitar at one time, I pretended it was. That the very thing I held in my hands once shot fire and smoke, and maybe even got a little blood splashed on it from Gene's wagging tongue. I didn't ask the guy if it was authentic, to me it already was. I hit the strings and ran my hand across the smooth surface, feeling the vibration as the solo to *100,000 Years* played in my head. Never before had I wanted to be Space Ace more than in that moment. I walked out of the store with my chest puffed out, proudly exhibiting my homemade shirt. I didn't care that almost all the glitter was gone, or that I probably smelled like dog piss, or that my face wasn't like anybody else's. I knew Ace was out there somewhere, walking the same planet as me, breathing the same air. And neither of us belonged.

30 - Flies to Shit

I stopped a man on the street who was walking toward me, book in his hand. I asked him if he knew where a used bookstore was.

"Over in Grand Junction there's a few. You might even find some medical dictionaries, with pictures and everything. I had myself a boil on my knee." The man pointed to one knee, then the other, like he couldn't remember which one. "That thing would squirt shit every time I ran. Hurt like a sonofabitch, too. But then I got me one of them medical dictionaries and treated it. Haven't had one since. And if I did I'd know exactly what to do, thanks to that book."

I thanked the guy and looked at my map. Grand Junction was the next town over, heading west. Maybe seven or eight miles away. The three burgers in my belly threatened to slow me down, but I kept at it and decided to walk instead of hitch. I'd be there before dark.

***

The walk made me thirsty. The road took me past a high school. I thought about running in and searching out a drinking fountain. But there was no way in hell. If I walked in that school it'd be a circus come to town. I think if I were crawling through the middle of the desert and a pool of cold water lay ahead surrounded by kids, I'd probably run in the other direction. It hurts to be honest sometimes, but maybe I'm a pussy.

As I passed by the school, I could see kids inside, sitting in their chairs, facing ahead. Then one of them saw me and, like flies to shit, the windows filled with wide eyes and pointing fingers. I picked up the pace and tried thinking about other stuff. About cherry sunburst guitars and libraries and wall-to-wall VHS tapes.

31 - An Attitude of Gratitude

I made it to Grand Junction just before sundown. I knew any bookstore would be closed, but I headed toward one anyway. I had asked a gas station employee for directions to the nearest. He said they only had one and drew me a map on a piece of paper. I bought a Mountain Dew and followed his directions. The bookstore was on the corner of Calhoun and Franklin, less than a mile away.

Nothing really stood out in Grand Junction. It wasn't as big as Denver or Boulder, but not as small as Golden. They had a nice little ice cream shop on the main strip, the windows covered in posters of banana splits, double and triple-scooped cones, Fudgsicles and snow cones. The kind of food you can't get out of a dumpster. Every bit of it looked good. But the stuff hurts my teeth so I passed on by.

I got to Calhoun Street right at dusk. The bookstore had a wooden sign out front that read *Rainbow Rick's*, next to it an engraved lion's head. The sign was old and most of the paint gone, but you could tell it cost the owner quite a bit when new.

The store was closed, right along with every other business nearby, with the exception of a gas station I could see up the road. The bookstore itself I nearly missed. I was looking for a small building, maybe a little storefront set in the middle of a plaza. But this was an old house. Every window in the place glowed amber, like a warm, inviting fire in each room.

I crept toward the house, walked up the porch steps. Each step gave a different creak. The slower I walked, the louder and more prolonged the wooden moan. I took the rest of the stairs quickly and stood on the porch, peeking through one of the windows.

It was beautiful. Shelves blocked most of my view, but I could make out enough to tell there was a wondrous maze inside made from pressed words that smelled of dust and yellowed pages. I wanted in. I headed back down the steps to look for a place to crash for the night. Somewhere near. I didn't get far before the bookstore's door opened and a little bell chimed.

"I saw you peeking."

I turned around, startled. There was a man standing there, hunched from age. He wore a brown cardigan that was unbuttoned with no shirt under it, just skin that clung loosely to his bones, peppered with long, gray hairs. The hair on his head matched his chest and stuck out wildly like he'd just woken up from a week-long sleep.

"Sorry," I said. "I was just looking at your setup. Looks like you've got a nice place here."

The man walked onto the porch and looked through the same window I had, then said, "You can't see jackshit from out here. Come on in," and shuffled slippered feet back inside, leaving the door open. I caught a glimpse of what I thought were underwear, as white as his hairless legs. But it was a diaper that made loud, plastic announcements when he walked. Announcements about getting old and being ashamed. I felt bad. I felt thankful.

The book smell hit me. Near overwhelming. Every few months, Sister Jude went to the library and brought back books that were donated to Gramm Jones. Those were some of my favorite days—if there was such a thing—and I always imagined a bookstore would smell a lot like those days.

I didn't want to leave the bookstore. I wanted to stay there for as long as it took for the smell to rub off on me, the smell of more books than the entire town would ever be able to read in a lifetime. And on bad days, I could maybe catch a whiff of the smell that would live in my old, dirty shirt and think of this moment while walking down the highway, waiting for mercy to pick me up and take me closer to Hermosa Beach where maybe I'd have my own little library of books one day.

The old man closed the door and the bell dinged above us.

"I'm Rick. This here is my kingdom, and I'm open just as long as there's a soul what needs a story. Now...what's your pleasure?"

I told him my name, said it was nice to meet him and asked if I could look around. He looked at my backpack, like maybe he wasn't sure if he could trust me. I caught on and took it off, set it by the front door. He smiled and opened his arm, inviting me to explore.

I saw stairs that led up to the next floor with books stacked on each step, leaving only a narrow path to navigate through. The amber color I'd seen from the outside came from lights that hung from the ceiling in each room. The kind that were popular fifteen years earlier, a long chain attached to gold velvet shades. They added warmth and character.

"May I ask what you like to read? This place is a jungle. Maybe I could help shorten your stay."

I didn't want to shorten my stay. I wanted to live there, carve out a bed in the shelves and read my life away, wear the cologne of aging pages. The place made Hermosa Beach feel like a plan B.

"It's easier to tell you what I don't like, I guess...I don't read nonfiction, and I'm not a big fan of war stories or love stories."

"No war stories, eh? You ever even read one?"

"Not really. I mean...I read *The Painted Bird* a few times, but I don't know if that's really a war story."

"Ahh, yes. *The Painted Bird.* That's not a book you see often. Hell, I don't even own a copy myself. Wish I did." I thought about giving him my copy, maybe trade him for something else. "How'd you manage to find one?"

It was one of the books the library had donated. I don't think they looked real close at what they gave away and to whom. If they had, there's no way in hell they'd hand that book over to a foster home.

"From the library."

"The library? Here in Grand Junction?"

"No, in Denver."

"Denver, eh? Is that where you're from?"

"Yeah, but I'm on my way to California." I knew he'd ask so I offered.

"Ahh, yes. The Sunshine State...or is that Arizona?"

I didn't tell him it was Florida.

"I had myself a woman in California for a spell, cute little miss. She liked it on top." He winked at me. "Anyway, back to painted birds and war stories. Follow me."

He led me to what I thought was the back of the store, until I saw two more rooms that branched off even further into other sections. Above each of the two doorways were white poster board signs with faded marker where someone had gotten creative. *SCI-FI* read one sign, a flying saucer floating near the letters and surrounded by stars. The other sign said

HORROR with a flaming hand covered in hair, sharp nails dripping with blood. We went in a different direction, and I took note of where the other two rooms were in case I got lost.

Rick fingered one of the shelves, looking for a specific book. I skimmed the titles and the authors. I recognized none of them.

"Here it is. This book right here will change your thoughts on war stories. Maybe open your mind a little. It's good to be diverse."

He handed me a hardback book with a shiny, protective jacket like most books from the Denver Public Library: *Some Kind of Hero* by James Kirkwood. I'd never heard of it, and the cover looked about as fun as an English textbook. I knew I wasn't going to spend my money on it, but I humored the guy and let him tell me a few things about it, including a lengthy rant about how they'd made a movie a few years ago based on the book and I should never watch that movie. Not ever. That it was a piece of shit that should have never been made.

I thanked him for pointing out the book and told him maybe I'd read it one day.

"I don't believe for a minute you'll read that book unless I drop it in your bag myself, so take it. Read it on your travels, young man. And when you do, think of me. Think of me and the bullet I took that caused this shitbag to hold my junk every hour of the day." He slapped his diaper, and it sounded like fire roaring and men dying.

"You sure?" I asked.

"Course I'm sure. Now let's get you back to the horror. I saw you being seduced by her."

He led me back to the horror room and told me to take my time, then went downstairs. The shelves were labeled by subgenre: Supernatural, Creatures, Medical, Occult, and something I'd never heard of before: Splatterpunk. It was a small shelf. Books from Barker, Schow, Lansdale, Skipp & Spector. I'd never heard of any of them. They were more expensive than the other books because they were new, but I wrote down the titles so I could look them up at the library in Hermosa Beach. I grabbed an old copy of *Tales of Edgar Allan Poe* that was falling apart and a book of *Rod Serling's Night Gallery* stories, then brought them downstairs.

The man was sitting behind a counter in a large, cushioned chair, his feet up, with a book in his lap.

"What'dya find yourself?"

I showed him the books. He gave me the Poe for a quarter and the Serling for fifty cents and reminded me to read the war story and to think of him when I did.

"Also, that's for you." The man pointed behind me to a corner of the store under the front windows. There was a sleeping bag laid out on the floor with a pillow, flashlight and a book next to them. "I can tell you've got no place to go. You stink worse than I do, and I don't mind putting you up for the night. I know you won't be stealing on me cuz I don't sleep. I read when I dream and I dream when I read." He gave me another wink.

"You sure you don't mind?"

"Levi, when a man says something, he should mean it. Always. The next time I say something where you're tempted to question whether I'm sure or unsure, save the words and know that I'm a man of mine. Now crack that spine and settle yourself in. Something tells me you haven't had the most restful nights as of late."

"You're right, Mr. Rainbow. I haven't. Thank you." I waited for him to tell me not to call him mister, but he didn't. Instead he said that Mr. Rainbow had a nice ring to it and that he liked it. Then he lit some candles, turned off the lights, and picked up the book he'd been reading and quietly read to himself.

I set my new books next to the sleeping bag and grabbed the book he'd set near the pillow. It was a book on the Boy Scouts of America. I had no interest in reading it, but I think Rick probably thought I could use it, maybe learn a thing or two about survival. I turned on the flashlight and opened the book. It creaked and snapped and whispered that it'd never been read before. That I was its first. I stared at the first page, not reading a word, just reflecting on the moment, the smell of the books, the soothing light of the candles, and the company of an old man who could teach the rest of the world a thing or two about generosity and kindness. So I stared at the page and reveled in an attitude of gratitude. I think Sister Jude would call my situation a blessing.

I put the book down and wrote Sister Jude a note on napkins, thanking her. I tried making a list of all the things I could remember that she'd done for me, but the list grew long and I ran out of napkins. So I went back to my book and finally broke through that first page, then the next, and kept reading until I fell asleep with the flashlight on.

I slept better than I think I ever had before, drunk from the smell of endless words on countless pages, as the books watched over me like God Himself, protecting me from a night filled with dreams of a parentless life in a loveless world that lies in wait for its next chance to reject my face. Rainbow Rick's was a blessing, alright. One I won't soon forget.

32 - One of the Good Ones

The sun woke me up. There was a thick beam that poured through one of the front windows. It highlighted the dust in the air. It looked like glitter. I looked down at my shirt. There were a few stains on it now, dirt mostly, maybe a dot of ketchup, too. I smelled my armpits. They were bad.

"I wish I could offer you a shower." Rainbow Rick said. He was still sitting in his chair, reading a different book than the night before. "Best I can do is give you a washcloth and bar of soap and send you upstairs to the sink. That's what I do. I wash all my goods. My pits, too. Though you get to be my age and your stink turns different. Not like when I was young. Hell, even then I didn't wear antiperspirant. That was our pheromone, that odor. You'd be surprised how much tail I got going au naturale."

Rick laughed. He was funny.

"You hungry?"

I was. But Rick's generosity made me feel uncomfortable, guilty. Like I was taking advantage of him. An old man who scooted around in a diaper, a headful of war stories.

"A little," I said.

"How about you go and get us some breakfast from the store down the road. I'll give you a list and some money." Rick stood and opened the register, took out a twenty-dollar bill and set it on the counter. Then wrote some things on a piece of paper. "If Helen's working, tell her I sent you and she'll give us some free coffee. She's a good woman, that one. Hell, if I were ten years younger I'd be all up in that." Then Rick laughed and wiggled his tongue quick like.

I went upstairs first and washed up, took a piss, then asked Rick which way to the store. He pointed which way and told me it was the 7-Eleven. Then he told me to leave my backpack here and that he was trusting me with his money because he thought I was one of the good ones.

***

I walked down the street and found the 7-Eleven easy enough. It turns out Helen was working. She was happy to give me a couple of free coffees when I dropped Rick's name. I went through the list he'd given me and grabbed everything: Powdered donuts, glazed donuts, a quart of milk, a pickle from the jar on the counter, and two bottles of orange juice.

As I stood in line, I noticed a little boy staring at me. He was holding on tight to his mother's hand, fear in his eyes. His mother was looking straight ahead at the clock, watching the second hand but not really. She'd already seen me and didn't dare turn my way again. She'd seen enough, and it was like that fear of hers spread right down through her hand and into the child. I wondered if the kid was by himself would he notice me at all. And if he did, would that fear still be there. I nodded at him and gave him the kindest eyes I could and tried real hard to smile. His brow furrowed and he buried his face in his mom's ass, peeking with one wide eye.

I paid for the food and left, making sure I got the receipt. And as I passed by a restaurant, I made a mental note to grab napkins after breakfast. I didn't like being without something to write on, and I wasn't ready to spring for a notebook. If anything, I needed a new shirt, or at least to clean the one I wore. Same with my pants. Every once in a while I caught a whiff of Britton's piss on them, when the wind blew just right.

When I got back to Rainbow Rick's I took a deep breath as I entered, anticipating the book smell. The bell chimed above the door, but the smell of books wasn't there. That euphoric aroma of pages was gone, like it'd been sucked out in a vacuum. Then I looked at Rick who still sat in his chair behind the counter. He was staring at the wall behind me. His eyes were red and glazed over, his face blue. Then I smelled the mess in his diaper and the vomit down his chest, clumped in the grey hairs under his cardigan.

I set the donuts and the milk on the counter and waited for Rick to breathe. I watched his chest closely, but the only movement was the slow trickle of what I guessed was orange juice and a few pills that never had a chance to break down. In his lap was a huge white book called *Aztec*. It was closed with a bookmark that stuck out from the middle of it.

I looked around for a phone. There wasn't one, not that I could see. I ran upstairs and looked. Every room was a world of books and nothing more. Even upstairs the smell of books was gone, like Rick had taken it with him. I went back downstairs and looked at him again.

This is my first dead body.

I remember thinking that, like maybe there were more to come between here and California. But I never wanted to see one again. Not ever. Rick's face was relaxed, almost stretched. And I swear his skin turned another shade of blue—gray, actually—in just those quick few minutes. His eyes were fixed to nothing, and I wondered what the last thing he ever saw was. The spot on the wall behind me? The pages of *Aztec*?

I grabbed my backpack and loaded in my four new books: *Some Kind of Hero*, the Rod Serling and Poe books and the Boy Scout book, then took out *The Painted Bird* and thought about why I didn't want to part with it. I could only come up with one reason: It was a part of my old life that maybe I didn't want to let go of. Part of Denver. Part of Sister Jude. I looked at the sticker on the spine and the stamp on the pages that said *Denver*

Public Library. I'd never even been there. And that was bullshit.

I stood and looked at Rick and thought about how different life was now, a lot different than when I first read that book. And I knew right then that I'd never read it again. When I was trapped in Gramm Jones it kept me going, knowing some kid out there had it worse than I could ever imagine. Even if he was fictional, I knew there were kids out there being beaten, raped, tied up, starved. But I wasn't.

I took the book and set it on Rick's lap next to *Aztec* and told him thank you. For everything. I couldn't bring myself to close his eyes like they do in the movies. If somehow he could still see me, like his spirit was hanging on until I left, I wanted him to know I really was one of the good ones. I wasn't there to steal.

I took the change from the twenty out of my wallet and set it on the counter. But I took the bag of food because I knew Rick wouldn't mind. He would have offered it and I'd ask him if he was sure.

And he would be.

33 - Skate to the Beach

I ended up back at the 7-Eleven and told Helen to call an ambulance. She started crying, and I couldn't handle it so I left. I sat in the carwash parking lot next door and drank my coffee, then left once I saw the ambulance pull up at Rainbow Rick's. I didn't head back down there. No reason to. I'd said my goodbyes.

I walked for probably ten miles before I ever stuck my thumb out. I needed to be alone. Nobody asking where I was going or where I was from or was I born this way. I zoned out the whole time and thought of Rick and his kingdom of books. He died doing what he loved. I decided I would read *Some Kind of Hero*, just for him.

***

When I did stick my thumb out, nobody picked me up and I made it to the next town, my legs weak, my appetite back. I had no idea where I was and didn't care. I'd check the map later.

I stopped at a park and sat at a picnic table, rummaged through my backpack for the donuts and ran across the food I'd gotten from McDonald's the day before. I dumped it all in the trash near the picnic table. I didn't trust it. I ate most of the donuts instead and downed them with the milk. It was warm, almost hot. But milk and donuts go too well together not to drink it.

While I was eating, a truck pulled up near the park and a guy with a mesh baseball cap got out, opened his tailgate, pulled two speakers out onto it and faced them toward me. The speakers were the kind you'd see hooked up to a home stereo in a living room, not in a truck.

The guy got back in the truck and turned on surf music—a soundtrack for California. It was loud, and I felt like it was just for me. I looked at the surrounding houses where women tended flower gardens and children played on swingsets, but nobody looked toward the truck. No one seemed to hear the reverbed guitar, the tribal toms. The music was surfboards and waves and sand and bikinis. It was Hermosa Beach in the 60s.

The man sat smoking a cigarette and sipping on what looked like a martini, right there in his truck. Occasionally he'd look at me and nod and I'd nod back. Finally, I got up and walked over to him. He smiled, raised his drink and then downed the rest of it.

"Want the olive?" He held it between his fingers, and when he spoke he pinched the olive with each syllable, as if the hole in the center was talking—a tiny green puppet.

"No thanks."

I asked him about the music and why he was playing it and was he playing it for me.

"I was," he said. "Your kind surf, right?"
My kind.

Until that moment I still carried doubt. That I was chasing after something that never was. Just an excuse to run away. But now it had to be real. There *was* someone else out there.

"Are you talking about Hermosa?"

"I'm talking about the waves, kid. You ride them?"

"No...I mean, not yet."

"Then maybe this ain't for you." The guy shut off the music, got out of his truck and pushed the speakers back inside, then closed the tailgate.

"Wait...do you know something about Hermosa Beach? Do you know a..." I didn't want to say it. I waited for him to interrupt me instead. He didn't. He just stared and waited. But he knew what the hell. "...a skullface man?" I finally said.

"Can't say as I have, though just between you and me and Penelope, here." He patted the back of the truck. "My old man has. And he's from the shore."

"Your dad saw someone like me?"

"I gotta go, kid. If I were you, I'd learn to surf." He got back into his truck, the rusted door was a dying crow.

"Wait." I'd never felt so desperate. "Can I talk to your dad? Will you give me a ride?"

"He's pushing daisies at Oak Hill Memorial and doesn't say much these days."

I asked him again for a ride.

"No can do. I'm headed to the pawnshop to get rid of these speakers. I could use a refill on the olives." He nodded toward the glove box where a jar of olives lay tipped on its side. There was one left. "If you're headed to the beach, I'd think about getting a skateboard. You'll look better gettin' there."

And then he drove away. That's when the women stopped their gardening and the children stopped their swinging. They got a good look at me and didn't quit until I moved along down the road and back on the freeway.

34 - Lessons on Love and Lycanthropy

I couldn't stop thinking about the guy with the speakers and all the questions I had. It drove me nuts. But what he did give me was even more drive to get to Hermosa.

I walked another five miles to the next town, Loma. I don't know if the whole town is a dump but everything I saw was. Paint-chipped houses with yards full of too much of nothing—old tires, pallets, sections of fence, rusted barbecues, and cinder blocks. Shit that hung around in case it was needed one day. But it never would be. I saw lots of trailers, too. Little campers and old RVs, like guest houses for knocked up daughters and their boyfriends too lazy or too stoned to get a job.

I could be wrong about that last part, but I don't think I am.

I was chugging on the OJ that I still had left, when I heard a "*pssst*" sound. I looked and saw a man crouched down behind a trailer, hiding. He was wearing nothing but a pair of cut off jeans that were way too tight and had the longest fringe I'd ever seen from old denim. That shit hung a foot past the cut. The guy's skin was the kind of dark tan that made his eyes bug out—even though they really weren't—and he had a short ponytail that should have never been, tied up with a shoelace.

"That bitch out there in her garden?"

I looked around, figured he was talking about the jungle of tomato plants across the street, and saw nobody there.

"I don't think so," I said.

"Careful, brother. She's ruthless. She sees you talkin' to me she'll think you're one, too."

Then something hit me hard in the chest, knocked the wind out of me. I'd been shot, was my first thought. I ducked behind the trailer with jean-shorts guy and clutched my chest, afraid to look.

"Haha! She got you good, brother."

I felt my chest. It was wet and messy, chunks of something stuck to me. *Guts?* I looked down, just barely, and out of my peripheral I could see the mess was red. And I remember thinking that if I'd been shot it didn't hurt as bad as I thought it would. Unless I'm in shock.

"You okay, man?" Jean-shorts asked, trying to stifle a laugh.

I looked at the mess on my hand. It was red, but not blood-red. I'd been hit with a tomato. And that thing sure didn't feel ripe. It felt like a rock, or a full can of Coke.

"She thinks you're one too."

"One of what?"

"A werewolf. It's her thing."

I looked at my shirt. There was a large wet spot in the center of my chest, stained pink-red.

Shit. I may have been homeless, but I didn't want to look it.

"She's been on me since the day I moved in. She says only gypsy wolfmen live in trailers. That no man in his right mind would wear his hair long, unless he couldn't help it. She said the devil was in me and I didn't even know it."

"You keep your wolfpack over there, young man! I don't want no trouble!" The old woman yelled, hidden among her plants.

"See? You keep walkin' down that way she's liable to throw all sorts of shit at you. You may wanna go back the way you came...or wait until dark."

"I can run," I said.

"Or you could come in and watch TV, drink a beer. I've got HBO."

I didn't know what HBO was, but he told me. Said they played uncensored movies. He emphasized there'd be nudity. T & A, he called it. I caught on.

A cold beer sounded good so I followed him in. The outside of the trailer looked a lot like my shirt—fading white, covered in dirt and tomato. The inside was cluttered with bowling trophies, candles and plants. There was a small bookshelf in the corner that held self-help books about plumbing and carpentry and electronics. I sat on the sofa while he poured beer from a 40-ouncer into coffee mugs. The beer was near flat but cold and felt good after all the walking. He turned on the TV and told me the T & A wouldn't show until later, after dark. We watched a few minutes of the movie that was on. I'd never seen it but recognized Barbara Streisand in it. A kid at Gramm Jones had a crush on her, used to have a picture of her on his wall. He even tried making a Barbara Streisand T-shirt after he saw my KISS one. It looked like shit, and I laughed and we got into it. I was being a dick, I know. That kid found a home soon after. I'd like to think maybe he has HBO now, wherever he is.

"I'm Chick," Jean-shorts nodded at me.

"I'm Levi." I extended my hand and he pretended not to see it, like he was too caught up in Barbara. "Thanks for the beer." I took a drink.

"No problem, brother. Glad you came around. I was bored. Was gonna plant some grass today...but that old bag ain't havin' it. I won't lose any sleep when she kicks the bucket." He sipped on his beer loud, like it was coffee or hot soup, then made an *aahhhh* sound. "So where you headed?"

"California."

"I knew you was going somewhere. I sense these things."

Sip. *Aahhhh.*

"So. Tell me, Levi. What are you runnin' from?"

I lied and told him I wasn't running from anything, that I had left home with the blessing of my mother to go stay with cousins where they had a job waiting for me at a video store. I hate lying.

"What I wouldn't give to be your age...how old are ya anyway?"

I told him.

"Hell yeah, sixteen and the world at your fingertips, your first love right around the corner. I don't suppose you've been in love though, have you?"

I was insulted, I guess. But it doesn't do me any good to have people pretend I'm something I'm not. I told him I hadn't been in love.

"Don't you fret. It'll happen. And it'll knock your dick in the dirt, too. And for a while you'll wish you never looked at a skirt in your life. But every man needs his heart broken at least once. It's like a big ball of shit whipped at you, and when it hits it stings like hell and smells, too. My God does it smell. And that smell doesn't go away, not for a long time. But then it starts to wash off and fade and then you realize that hidden under all that shit was another ball, and that ball was wisdom, but it didn't splatter...it seeped in you. Right to the core of you. And it ain't ever going away. That ball stays with you and you use it. Trust me."

Sip. *Ahhhhh*.

"There's an old saying...It's best if you fall in love and then lose them than to have never loved somebody...something like that. Someone famous said it. Eastwood or some shit. Maybe Bronson.

Hell, I don't know. You get it, though. And I can tell you'll find her one day. I sense these things."

There was a thud on the side of the trailer. I jumped, nearly spilling my beer.

"Bitch throwin' fruit again...did you know tomato was a fruit? I didn't know that. Read it in a book when my electricity went out. Who'da thought?"

Sip. *Ahhhh.*

"She may do that for a while. We can duck out and I can show you around. Or we can stick around and play some cards. But just so you know, that fruit hitting the house gets on your nerves after a bit."

"Can't you just call the police?"

"I'd rather not have them digging around here. Let's just say, she's not the only one growin' plants."

Another tomato hit the trailer.

"Let's get outta here...grab your beer."

Chick led me to a back bedroom in the trailer, parted a curtain and stuck his head through a screen that may as well not been there at all, then we both climbed through and hit the ground.

We walked down a side road paved with dirt, then through a patch of trees where a giant rock sat next to a stream. It was peaceful, the trickle of the stream over rocks. The water was shallow and you could see the sandy bottom. I wanted to put my feet in it, wiggle the sand between my toes. But I didn't.

A breeze picked up through the trees and with it came an unpleasant odor I couldn't place. Then it was gone and I could smell the water and the grass again. I wished I was alone out there with my pen and my napkins and the trickle. It would get me writing something real nice. Maybe even some poetry.

"I wanted to show you something, Levi. And in turn, I'm hoping you can help me...and let me know I'm not crazy. That I'm not the beast that bitch says I am."

Chick pointed to the other side of the rock.

"Tell me I'm not a monster...that this isn't savage."

I looked. A set of blackened feet with red polish on the toes poked out from behind the rock.

I crept closer.

Lying face down, with its head in the water, was a body. Naked. A corpse, decomposing. The carcass was bloated like a balloon, like if you poked it with something sharp it might pop. It was speckled with blacks and browns and yellows, and there were deep cuts on its back filled with maggots. A breast bulging out the side told me it was a woman. Her long blonde hair pulsed hypnotically in the water with the current, giving an eerie beauty to the rotting thing. And then the smell came again, and I ran.

"I'm not a monster! I'm not a wolfman!" Chick screamed from behind me.

As the branches and the grass made their sound against my legs, I imagined it being Chick in full wolf form, galloping toward me, claws extended. And knew if I made it out alive it'd make a hell of a thing to write about.

I never ran that fast. Probably never will again. Chick's screams became distant and I hit another clearing, then saw a road up ahead. A different road than the one we'd taken. I had no problem with that. I'd follow it until I got another ride and got the hell out of Loma.

Then I realized I didn't have my backpack. I'd left it at the trailer.

35 - A Roadside Plan

Part of me was screaming no way in hell. The other part reminded me I didn't leave Gramm Jones to play it safe and that this was all an adventure. Every bit of it. I needed to go back to Chick's and get my backpack. I knew Chick was batshit crazy, probably a murderer too, and that the police needed to get involved. But not yet. I still couldn't be sure my disappearance from Gramm Jones hadn't been reported, that someone out there wasn't looking to put me back in the system. So I sat in the trees and devised a plan.

36 - Under the Moonlight

I spent most the day in the woods, bored as shit, killing time. It didn't take long to find Chick's place. Now I just needed to wait for nightfall. I was banking on two things: Either he'd head out, maybe hit a bar, go bowling, whatever the hell. Or he'd pass out drunk. The amount of empties in his trailer said he liked to drink.

The wait was hell. I was starving. Even the tomatoes looked good. And had I thought the old woman wouldn't give me away, I would have snatched one or two.

I hid in the tall grass across the road from Chick's and wrote in my head while I waited. It was the worst time I'd had since leaving Gramm Jones, and while I sat there among the itchy grass and invading bugs, I thought of ditching the plan and hitting the road, leaving my books and all of my writing behind. But then I thought about what my next entry would say—my first new one. It wouldn't start with an adventure but a confession, about being a pussy.

After dark, I moved from the grass to behind Chick's trailer. I could hear his TV and occasionally the erotic moans that accompany "T & A" films. The glow of the TV pouring through the windows and bouncing off the trees was comforting somehow, and for a little while kept my mind off food.

I sat there for hours, dozing off more than once, and waited for Chick to leave. Or go to bed. I'm not sure what time it was when the television glow stopped and the house went silent, but when it did I moved my position under the bedroom window where the open screen was all but gone, and I listened while Chick readied for bed. I sat there for at least an hour in complete silence before starting my search for a boost to the window. I figured the front door would be locked and I'd have to climb through.

I searched around the trailer and found nothing I could step on. I made my way to the old woman's house and found a hollow log she'd been using as a flower pot. I tipped the log and rolled it across the street, behind Chick's trailer and under his window. I waited another half hour before stepping on the log and peeking through. The moon cast a beam through the trees and across Chick's bed. He was sprawled out, naked and snoring.

I looked back at the moon. It wasn't full, but close. And I wondered if it were full would Chick still be there. Or would his naked ass be out on the prowl for another woman to do whatever it was he did to the other. And how many others were there?

I boosted myself up and through the window, the screen ripping around me. Chick didn't stir.

Not even a little. Heavy alcohol consumption was really the only thing there was to stop him from waking as I climbed through only a few feet from him.

While stuck in the window—half in, half out—I stepped outside myself, saw my ass sticking out the window of a trailer in the middle of the night, breaking and entering, and thought about the stereotype I was fulfilling: Troubled foster kid turned criminal. And I thought about how disappointed Sister Jude would be. Missing backpack or not. But my whole life has been about surviving. We all have our own shit to deal with, our own storms to battle through. And this was mine. And it called for action that some might not approve of. But that backpack wasn't just some sentimental bag of throwaways. My whole life was in that bag.

I pushed further into the room. Below me was a gap between the wall and the bed, but too far to drop without crashing to the floor. I reached out to the bed, put my weight on it. Slowly. The room was filled with alcoholic breath and Venetian moonlight. And as I eased down onto the floor, my fear left me. I stood at the foot of the bed and watched Chick breathe undeservedly. And if I'm to tell the truth, I had a moment of vigilante justice run through me—just a moment of it—as I spotted a baseball bat in the corner of the room and wondered how many women I might save.

Then Chick moaned and shifted. I stood stone still—a skull-faced gargoyle at the end of a killer's bed. His snoring resumed and I slowly backed into the hallway. I was in the clear. My backpack sat there on the floor where I'd left it. I unzipped it, made sure it still contained the books, the napkins. There was a box of crackers and a pack of smokes on the coffee table. I stared at them, pretending I was only slightly tempted, that maybe I wouldn't steal them. But I knew I would. And I did. I became the stereotype. The crackers are obvious. Shit, I was starving. The cigarettes? I decided as soon as I saw them I was gonna start smoking. A stupid habit to pick up when you've got no means to buy more, but they'd help pass the time.

I took the stuff and headed out the door and thought about how the tomato on the trailer looked like blood under the moonlight.

37 - The Best Thing I Ever Smelled

I found a payphone later that night, called the police and left an anonymous tip. Told them the whereabouts of the woods and near what street. I mentioned the stream and the rock and said I thought a guy named Chick did it and gave the best description of his trailer I could. It wasn't hard. They had questions but I hung up. I had no answers.

I didn't sleep that night, but I did finally eat. I downed half the box of crackers then stopped because the shit just sat there in my throat, begging for water. For anything to wash it down. I found a ride about an hour after hitting I-70. The ride was uneventful. A suit-and-tie guy picked me up. He kept the radio on, playing soft rock hits from the 70s. I dozed against the window for an hour until the guy woke me up, told me this was it and dropped me off in the parking lot of a motel while he went and got himself a room.

I hit the road, searched for lights, anything that might look like a store or a fast food joint still open. I thought of going into the motel and asking for water, but there was a drunk in the office bitching about his room smelling like perfume and if his wife smells it on him he's coming back to sue. So I moved on and let the crackers sit there.

The clock in Suit-and-Tie's car had read 4:06. I walked a little, then sat on the side of the road, wrote until I heard the birds waking up, then trudged on. Up ahead, lights flickered. They were coming from a small building surrounded by nothing but empty land and a few parked cars. It was a diner. An old rundown piece of shit I could smell a quarter-mile away. It was the best thing I'd ever smelled.

38 - Everything I've Ever Needed

The diner was called "Dottie's". There was only one other person in there—an old man at the counter hovered over a cup of coffee. I took a seat in a booth, my backpack next to me. A woman named Lucille handed me a menu and told me she was sorry but they were out of bacon. I told her that was fine, then ordered pancakes and water.

"Water?" she said. She looked at my backpack and at my shirt. And maybe she smelled me, too. "Honey, are you ordering water 'cause you don't think you can afford milk?"

I said "Yes ma'am." And she said "I'm bringing you milk. Don't you worry about it...and hash browns, too." She wrote stuff on a pad and ripped the page off on her way to the back where she slapped it down on a little counter that opened into the kitchen, then rung a bell and shouted, "stack of cakes and browns!"

The diner smelled of old cigarettes and fried food dipped in coffee. Another man strolled in and parked at the counter. I could tell this was a regular stop for some—a second home for the lonely.

After Lucille topped the men's coffee, she caught me writing on a napkin. My last one. I'd be grabbing a few before I left.

"Whatchya writing?"

I told her I was keeping a journal of my travels. Then she asked me where I was headed. I told her, but not why.

"Honey, you need a proper notebook, maybe one of those little leather-bound journals. I don't have either, but you can use this."

She pulled a pad of tickets from her apron and handed it to me. The tickets said *Guest Check* at the top, each page lined and numbered. You've seen them. I thanked her, and she set a small glass of water in front of me. I drank it quick, washed down the crackers.

Lucille went back to the counter and I stuffed my napkins in the backpack, took to writing on the pad. Perfect. Other than a comfortable bed, I was right where I wanted to be: In a shithole diner, engulfed in a cloud of coffee breath, stale smoke, and cooking grease.

I emptied out my backpack, took out my books and stacked them, thumbing through each one. I wrote my name in the backs of them. This was my library.

Lucille brought me the pancakes and milk and hash browns that I smothered in ketchup. She had a big heart, that woman. I ate every bit of the food and drank the whole glass of milk. By the time I was done I had to unbutton my pants.

I opened the smokes I'd stolen from Chick, lit one with a book of matches I got from a bowl that sat on the counter next to the coffee drinkers. I took a hit and added to the cloud the other men had summoned. I inhaled deeper than I should have and coughed enough to draw all eyes to me. I took a smaller hit next time and inhaled carefully. It burned my throat but felt good somehow.

I took note that the walls were covered in license plates. Utah license plates. I'd made it out of Colorado. I pretended I was smiling and thought about Gramm Jones and how it can go to hell. This new freedom was everything I've ever needed.

39 - Playing A Round

Lucille wouldn't let me pay for the food. I tried, but she wasn't having it. I wanted to give her something, but other than a book from my library, I had nothing to offer. If I were an artist, I'd draw something. If I were poet, I'd write a sonnet, give it to her. I told her I wished there was something I could do to repay her for her kindness. She said, "I wouldn't have it any other way, honey."

I slipped two dollars under my plate as a tip and left before she told me no.

***

I found myself in a small town I never caught the name of. I walked through it, dipped into some shops. I got some stares but people seemed nice enough. I found one store that had a rack of clothes outside on the sidewalk. I thought of stealing a shirt, maybe some pants, but my life as a petty thief was a one-time incident (the garage sale doesn't count). And if you ask me, I say stealing from Chick was justified.

I took to a McDonald's bathroom and cleaned up the best I could, then bought a few hamburgers and some fries for later. I knew the stomach full of too many pancakes and half a plate of hash browns wouldn't stick around. Food sure doesn't last as long as you need it to some days.

I felt safe in Utah, an invisible border between myself and Gramm Jones. If I'd slept the night before I wouldn't have minded walking most the day, but between the diner food and nothing but a quick nap against a car window, I was sluggish. Content but slow.

I found a golf course and strolled along the fairway. Some angry yuppie with money to burn left a club in the grass, bent it out of frustration from a bad drive that landed his ball in the woods. I watched him do it. I kept my distance, then grabbed the club, did my best to straighten it, then made myself at home on the course. There were plenty of balls in the brush and I grabbed a bright yellow one, pretended I knew what the hell and hit the ball from green to green. Golf wasn't as fun as I thought it'd be. Not alone, anyway. After a few hours of hitting the ball and chasing it down, I knew golf wasn't for me.

I went from exhausted to dead tired and crashed out in some tall grass behind a line of trees and didn't wake up until the birds did the next day.

40 - Smoking Peace

I woke refreshed and hungry. Lit a smoke and practiced inhaling, carefully. It wasn't quite dawn yet, but getting there. I wanted to read or write but couldn't see. The moon had taken off, and the sun was taking its time.

There was something about the smokes that gave me peace of mind. It was a reminder that it was just me and the world, not me and the cage that is Gramm Jones. It was a reminder that I wasn't the runt in a litter of orphans. I was in my late teens. Late. And it felt good to have a vice. One that didn't slow down my ambitions or leave me incoherent and acting a fool.

As the sun began casting shadows, I made my way off the course and to the street. I checked the map and headed south with a nicotine buzz and a new walking stick.

41 - Robert & the Grand Canyon

The minute I hit the freeway I got a ride. She was an elderly woman, eyes inches above the steering wheel. I don't know what scared me more, the drunk back in Boulder or this woman.

When I hopped in, she called me Robert and told me if I wanted any gum that she had some in her purse. She said it was my favorite, *Black Jack.*

"I'm taking you home, Robert," she said. "I doubt your mother knows you're out here...in the wild."

I figured as long as she stays on I-70 we're okay. She talked to me about brothers and sisters that weren't mine, about how my mother embarrassed her last Thanksgiving when she wouldn't let her cut the turkey and how she should have more respect for her elders. Then she would point out landmarks, buildings and such where she used to roller skate. She pointed to an abandoned gas station and told me she saw The Beatles play there once, gave Paul McCartney a hickey on his neck.

Then she screamed and said, "Who the hell are you?" Like seeing me for the first time.

I told her my name and where I was headed and not to worry because I'd never hurt her, that I was just looking for a ride.

"I'm not worried. But your mother is, I'm sure. You can't do this to her, Robert," she said.

This went on for a while, maybe an hour. Then she stopped on the side of the road and asked if I'd take her picture.

"I've always wanted my picture taken in front of the Grand Canyon," she said, then handed me a small camera and told me to keep taking pictures until I couldn't. She stood on the side of the road and looked out over the flat land and sighed heavily.

"It's beautiful! Hurry….take one of me seeing it for the first time!"

I snapped a picture. It was sad. Slowly, but as fast as her old bones would allow, she laid on the ground and propped her head up with her hand, posing.

"Take another, Robert."

I did. I took several. And I wondered when she got them developed what she would see. A crazy old lady looking out over the flattest land God's ever made and wonder who in the hell took the photo? Or would she look upon them fondly, sticking them in an album full of other nonsense, pictures taken by strangers named Robert.

I took pictures until there were no more to take. Then she stood very still, and with her arms spread out said, "Robert...if I jump, will you catch me?" She was looking at the ground. Her eyes fixed five feet away to a safe landing of pebbles and dirt. "Will you catch me, Robert?"

"Don't jump." I said. "You've made it this far."

She turned around and looked at me, told me I was right, then asked me who the hell I was. Before she called me Robert again, I gave her the camera and led her back to the car, then walked away. She drove off with my walking stick, and I could barely make out the top of her hair over the seat, like a ghost behind the wheel.

42 - Centerfolds & Smokes

Utah may be beautiful to some, but not to me. Not the parts I saw. I saw flat desolation. So when a trucker picked me up heading southwest down I-70 I was more than happy to join him. The soundtrack was awful—twangy songs about boozing and losing. But the conversation was pleasant, and as the hours went by I grew nervous knowing how close I was getting to California.

The trucker's name was Little Gene. He must have been near 300 pounds, most of it in height, and the truck's cab was decorated in Playboy centerfolds. From all twelve months, he told me. He showed me his favorite. Miss October—a blonde with dark, Brooke Shield eyebrows and blue eyes. She was pretty, and as I looked at them all she became my favorite, too.

Little Gene talked a lot about life on the road, and we traded stories. I told him about Chick and the girl by the stream. He said the "sumbitch" should fry for it. I agreed.

I told him about Lori and Hannah and Scottie. He said Utah is full of crazy love triangles and said he hoped those poor women got away 'cause that shit never works.

When Little Gene lit up a smoke I did too—two men on the road, miles behind us, miles ahead. Surrounded by flat ugly land and beautiful T & A. This was the life.

43 - Deep West

We got a break from the flat land and trekked through what I suppose Utah called mountains. Ugly rock plateaus and jagged cliffs. Nothing like what Colorado offered. We were deep west now. Desert territory. And Vegas was just ahead. Disneyland for the debaucherous. I couldn't wait. I'd seen the pictures, the films. Vegas was a man-made star on earth. An ever-brilliant light that traded shifts with the sun.

Little Gene's cab was full of munchies—chips, beef jerky, donuts, and warm pop. He told me to help myself, that he needed to start eating better but that a young man like myself can handle living off junk. He said that it isn't until you get older that you've gotta watch it. He said it while patting his gut. A stomach that hid away a belt, one that probably had a buckle with his name on it. Or maybe a pair of brass tits.

I stuffed myself with the junk food. And with bladders full of pop, we parked on the side of the road and emptied out.

"Check it out, Levi." Little Gene nodded down the road toward a sign. It said *Welcome to Arizona!* Seven days I spent trying to get out of Colorado. It was only yesterday I hit Utah, and here I am saying goodbye already. Little Gene said we were at the very corner of Arizona and that if we had to piss bad enough we could push it from here to Nevada, that's how close we were.

When we got back in the rig I told Little Gene I had $3.25 and he was welcome to it. I told him it wasn't much but I wanted to show my gratitude. I was grateful for the ride, the food, and the normalcy. He chuckled and said I offered a break in the monotony and I was doing him some good by getting rid of the food and that let's face it, a gut like his wasn't gonna be snatching up no Miss October.

For the most part, Utah was good to me. I got myself a belly full of diner food, a writing pad, some smokes, played some golf, and Little Gene said if it wasn't for me that more women may have died. Still, good riddance, Utah.

44 - Worst-Case Scenarios

Little Gene was right. I'm not sure fifteen minutes went by before we were being welcomed into Nevada. I finally told him why I was headed to California. He said if he wasn't on the clock then he'd take me straight to the beach. I believed him. So far, Little Gene was the best friend I'd ever had.

"So, do you think this guy is your dad?" he asked me.

"I don't know," I said. "I can't tell if it seems like the logical thing or I just want it so bad that I can't see my way around it."

"Either way, Levi, I think the road is helping you find yourself. It's helped me. Hell, I've been flattenin' this tar since I was twenty. That's a lot of miles, a lot of time to think. And a whole a lot of life experience. It sounds to me like even this past week has put you years ahead of the rest." He reached up, honked the horn for a kid in the next lane who was frantically making the motion with his arm. The kid smiled real big after Little Gene let him have it. "I'm proud of you for steppin' out, taking life by the balls. Even if you don't like what you find at the end of the road." He honked for another kid in the passing car who'd missed it the first time. "You gotta learn to keep in mind a worst-case scenario. Because when it comes down to it, it's never as bad as you think. Sometimes it takes saying out loud our biggest fear. That's when we find there ain't nothin' to fear at all."

I thought hard about Little Gene's words. Sometimes it takes another's perspective to help line up your own.

We stopped at a diner called *The Desert Rose*. It wasn't as run down as the one in Utah, but it smelled the same, maybe a little more smoke and more seats taken. Little Gene ordered us grilled cheese sandwiches, tomato soup and apple pie. He ate his pie in a bowl of milk so I did too. It was good. Real good. I offered to pay for mine, at least for some of it, but Little Gene said it was reward for keeping him company. Then we lit smokes and talked about gambling and how it's a dangerous thing. He told me he hit the casinos every time he found himself in Vegas but that he had a limit, and that limit came about because of bad decisions the first time he was there. He said never again would he find himself in that position. He made me promise if I ever found myself standing in the middle of all that money that I'd set a limit too, and that win or lose I'd stick with it.

"Tonight, when we get to Vegas, I'm gonna do what I always do. I'm gonna hit the slots and the tables, and maybe grab myself a piece of ass. I like to treat myself to a room now and again. The sleeper gets a little cramped. So I want you to have it for the night, Levi. You can clean it free of snacks if you like and just relax yourself and read one of them books of yours. I don't imagine I'll be back until noon tomorrow, and from there I'm heading to dropoff and then back East. But tonight she's all yours."

It felt good to be trusted. It felt good to have a mutual respect for someone. But knowing I probably wouldn't see Little Gene again after that night took some of the joy away.

45 - Highway to Hell

On the way to Vegas, Little Gene let me pick the radio station. I couldn't find anything I liked, so he told me to reach under the seat, said there was a tape under there. It was the only tape he had. He said it was there when he got the rig but never listened to it, said he meant to but never got around to it. I found it: *AC/DC*. It was still wrapped in cellophane.

"Highway to Hell," I read aloud.

We both chuckled at the irony. I'd heard of the band, just never heard them. I opened it, put it in. It was heavier than KISS, heavier than Alice. It was a whole other level of rock. Pissed off, testosterone fueled, horny, and raw. I was in love. And judging by the tapping of Little Gene's meaty fingers on the steering wheel, I think he was too. The tape flipped twice by the time we got to Las Vegas.

46 - Arrival & Departure

It was dark by the time we pulled into Vegas. You could see the glowing beast miles ahead. Arriving at night is an experience all its own. Something daylight would ruin. Like Halloween under the sun. You don't trick or treat after walking out the door with a belly full of lunch. You hit that shit when the sky goes dark, the ghoulish shapes of a hundred kids spotlighted by only the glow of porch lights and jack o' lanterns.

The city was a sensory overload.

Little Gene couldn't take the rig down a main strip so we drove parallel to one, and I could see the oddly shaped hotels and casinos with lights that shouted *Pick Me!* Buildings filled with too much oxygen and people experiencing their best days, and far too often their worst. Beautiful car crashes with victims that sometimes walked away stripped of financial worry, or maimed for life, leaving their families with second mortgages and empty cupboards.

We parked in the empty lot of an abandoned gas station. It was on the corner of an intersection and gave a straight shot to the action.

Little Gene grabbed a small suitcase from inside the sleeper, opened it, rummaged through it. He checked over each item: a change of clothes, electric razor, cologne, and a Playboy magazine.

"I really do read the articles too, ya know." Little Gene said with a smile.

He closed the case and looked at me. His face wore concern and something somber.

"You're a helluva road companion, Levi." He paused. "Oh...I nearly forgot!"

He scrunched down and reached back into the sleeper, searching for something, then handed me two paperback books full of wear and dog ears and said "For your library."

He pointed to one. "This one here is the first James Bond book. I think you'll like it. The other is just to pass the time. It's not great, but you can't fault a book with a cover like that."

The cover showed a busty redhead sporting a Viking helmet. She was naked.

We shook hands, then he stepped down from the rig with his suitcase. "May the rest of your trip be free of werewolves and dumpsters, my friend...and I'd better not find any munchies in here when I get back. Fill that backpack of yours. I mean it. Deliver me from temptation." Then he made a little clicking sound with his tongue against his teeth, gave me a wink and shut the door.

I watched as he walked down the road toward the lights and hoped he'd come back with a wallet full of winnings. He deserved it.

47 - A Lizard Named Starr

I didn't stay in the cab. I had to see Vegas. I wasn't interested in the casinos but the nightlife, the culture. The idea that it truly never slept. But as I walked through the beautifully lit streets, the town felt like nothing but a last resort, somewhere you went while you died inside, with sex and money to fill the void. The prostitutes lingered, and the nude clubs stood in spots casinos wouldn't fit. If a man wasn't getting a blowjob in an alley, he was crying in a beer over the money he'd lost. It was a novelty. It was dismal. And I knew the number of people who could take it or leave it were few. The rest were looking for happiness, but like a dog that returns to his vomit, these people returned to something they continually believed offered them happiness. This was my impression, which was later confirmed when I met a miserable guy named Tommy and his sister, Starr.

I'd just turned the corner of a street, heading back to the rig, when I caught the attention of three guys. Jock types in their early twenties. They started in on the regular shit: Freakshow jokes. Nothing new. I ignored them like I tend to do. But whether it was the fault of alcohol or that empty void I was talking about, these guys followed me with their insults, then cornered me.

"What in the hell are you supposed to be, boy?" said the tallest of them, an Oxford shirt buttoned down to expose muscles I wished I had. He seemed to be the leader of the group. The other two just grunted in agreement and laughed when cued.

I said nothing. There was nothing to say.

"I asked you a question, skeleton kid! What the hell are you?"

"I'm the kid who's gonna break your face with mine." Which meant a good ole' headbutt. I'd used the line before, but not against three guys at once. I'd dug a grave.

Oxford sunk a fist into my stomach and I dropped. It's the only place I'd ever been punched, the stomach. A bullseye target. Even these assholes knew knuckle against bone wasn't a good idea. One of the laughers kicked me in the ribs and I found myself fetal-ing up. A humiliating position if you've ever been there. It lets you and everyone else know what a pussy you are, that you've given up.

"Tommy! What the hell?!" A woman's voice.

The three stepped back and I peeked. A slim figure in a tight black dress was speed-walking toward us—barefoot, heels in her hand.

"That does it, Tommy! I'm telling Mother."

Tommy changed. His pride disappeared. His friends walked away, deserting him.

"I was just kidding, Sis. He's fine. See? Get up, kid."

I didn't. I played the victim. Not because I was scared but because I wanted to see where this was going. I wanted to see just how much my cowering got him in trouble with Mother.

"Get up," he said through gritted teeth. He cocked his leg to land another kick.

I balled up even more, covering my face again. A gutless turtle.

I heard the familiar sound of a Polaroid camera, the kind they'd use at Gramm Jones when a new kid came in—somber faces caught in the act of not having a family, then tossed in a file and buried with others.

"Shit! Please don't, Starr. I was just playing around."

"No you weren't. I saw you. And now Mother will too."

"I'm sorry, kid."

I peeked again. He had his hand out. Kissin' ass. I stood up on my own, brushed myself off. The girl was shaking the Polaroid picture. I didn't want it to exist—me on the floor, acting a pussy.

"Get out of here, Tommy."

The guy hung his head, feet stomping down the walk. He wasn't tough anymore. He was just an asshole. The girl walked up to me. Mid-twenties, beautiful, empathetic eyes. Long dark hair.

"I'm so sorry. Are you okay?" She put her hand on my shoulder. "He's such a dick sometimes."

I told her I was fine. She looked at my shirt, squinted.

"I *love* KISS," she said. "Who's your favorite?"

"Ace."

"I used to like Paul, but now I'm in a Peter phase. I just love his voice."

She stuck the Polaroid camera in a purse that was too small for it. It stuck out the top. Then she put her heels on. She looked like a "lot lizard," as Little Gene called them.

"Can I ask why you took that picture?"

"Blackmail. Our mother pays his tuition. He's in his second year at UCLA. Psychology if you can believe that. She's on the verge of cutting him off, which if you ask me she should have done a long time ago. I mean...who wants an asshole like that for their psychologist, you know? If she knew half the shit Tommy did she'd leave him high and dry...like she did me." She pulled a smoke from her purse, offered me one. Mine were in the rig. We both lit up and I let her keep talking. "I've told her for years he's nothing but trouble, but she's got this idea that he's a little angel and I'm the jealous one who can't get her shit together. Trust me...there's no jealousy." She exhaled. A lipstick scar on her cigarette. "What's your name?"

"Levi."

"That's a cool name. I like it. I'm Starr."

She took two pennies out of her purse and handed me one, then pointed at a fountain and said, "Make a wish." She walked over to it and closed her eyes, her mouth moving slightly, mumbling a secret wish. Then she tossed the penny into the fountain and watched it disappear among the others.

"Come here and make a wish."

I humored her, and she smiled like a kid does when you hand them candy.

"So, what's your story?" she asked.

I told her I was just passing through on my way to Hermosa Beach.

"California? Are you driving there?"

"No. I've been hitchhiking."

"I hate hitching rides. It's dangerous. It's how I got out here. But I'll never do it again. I came here to make money." She kinda frowned when she said it. I was right. She was a hooker. "And before you ask, I'm no cokehead. I'm saving for school." She flicked her cigarette and got another. I was still babying mine.

"What about your mom? Isn't she paying for your brother?" I asked.

"My mother disowned me when I got pregnant. I lost it." She rubbed her belly, caressed it like there was still something there. But there wasn't. "She thinks I got an abortion. But I didn't, Levi. I wouldn't have done that. I would have given that baby a good home, a loving home, you know?"

"Isn't there another way you can get money? You seem pretty smart."

"Hell yes I'm smart. I've been accepted to three different universities. But brains don't pay for tuition. Not in my case anyway...You have any idea how much I make a week?" I shook my head. "No less than two thousand bucks. Men are pigs, you know?"

"Sorry."

"Don't be. I've been saving money all year. I figure come the new year, I'm gone. And I'll leave every bit of this behind me. This doesn't define who I am." She tugged at her dress. "It took me a while to believe that, but it's been my mantra all summer. And when I have the money and I'm in school, preparing for my future...one that I built on my own...I won't give a single thought to this past year. I'll erase it, like it never happened." She dug through her purse while she talked. "And when I tuck my kids in at night and lie in bed with my husband and talk about our blessings, I'll go to sleep knowing I did everything I could to make it happen."

Starr had all the confidence in the world. She believed every word she said. But something told me things wouldn't go as planned and that one day those demons might come back to haunt her, and when she looked her husband in the eye she'd see every man she never wanted to touch and it'd kill the passion. Sex would become a chore that felt like a tiresome necessity.

She looked at me, tilted her head and put her hand on my face, running her thumb along my cheekbone, then looked at her thumb and said, "Glitter! Where'd this come from?"

I looked down at my shirt. Every bit of the glitter was gone now. Starr held the last piece under her bright pink nail.

"My shirt. It used to have a lot more."

"I see. Come on. I'm buying you dinner," she said.

"You don't need to do that. I've got food."

"I didn't ask if you had food. I'm enjoying your company, and I'm buying you dinner. Now come on." She tugged at my hand, holding it as we walked. "Where to?"

I told her I wasn't picky, anywhere was fine.

"Do you like Chinese?"

"I've only had it once," I said.

She let go of my sweaty hand and lit another smoke, offered me one. I took it. We walked for three blocks, a path lit by the multi-colored Las Vegas sun. Hotels, casinos, tourist shops. Cars slowed near us, horny business men with wives at home, asking if she was open for business, declaring the party was in their car as they'd roll out bags of white powder. Bait. Starr ignored them and pretended her life was normal. More than once her eyes met those of other women, trading bitter looks and silent judgments. I hate to admit it, but it felt good not being the center of attention. Those looks, those slowing cars. None of them were for me.

***

The restaurant was a buffet, something else I'd never done. The carpet was red, the trim black. The decor and the employees reflected Chinese culture. We sat in the far back and smoked our cigarettes until it was time to hit the buffet. Starr helped me pick stuff to eat. I couldn't tell what most of it was. I told her I didn't want anything with eggs, but she talked me into trying an eggroll, told me it didn't taste like eggs and that I'd like it. She was right.

We ate. We smoked. We talked about the usual stuff: Where I was headed and why. It gets old talking about myself, but some people like Little Gene and Starr really take interest. They're good listeners.

The food was the best I think I'd ever had. With the exception of Thanksgiving and Easter, the food at Gramm Jones was only to sustain the kids, keep them alive and healthy. Never for pleasure. Lots of white rice. Lots of broccoli. The buffet had a fair share of those, too, but they were complimented. The Chinese know their shit.

For nearly an hour we talked. Then I told her I should go, that I was leaving early tomorrow. I thanked her for the meal and she thanked me for the company and for being a gentleman and not asking about prices or whether or not she did butt stuff.

48 - She Meant Well

I slept good. The sleeper was comfortable, but I could see how Little Gene would grow tired of it. The clock on the dash said 7:10 when I woke up. I ate some donuts and drank a warm pop, lit a smoke and read *Some Kind of Hero* and thought of Rainbow Rick. An hour later I'm stuffing my backpack full of my new books, the chips, the beef jerky, and the donuts, and there was a knock on the passenger side door. It was Starr. Her hair was in a ponytail. She wore a pair of tight faded jeans and a plain T-shirt. No makeup, no purse, no heels. She looked beautiful. I opened the door and she hopped in, bounced on the seat excitedly.

"Good morning, Levi."

I asked her how she found me. She said she followed me last night and told me she only did it because she was hoping to catch me before I left, that she had a gift for me. She handed me a black cloth rolled up in her fist and said, "Open it."

I unrolled it on my lap. It was a T-shirt. A KISS T-shirt. The cover of KISS Alive to be exact—the band in live-action poses, surrounded by smoke and colored lights.

"I used to wear it, but not for a long time now. I thought you'd appreciate it more. Besides, you can hardly see Peter."

"I don't even know what to say."

"Say you need coffee, cuz I sure do."

I took my old shirt off, put the new one on. It fit perfect but smelled of perfume. I didn't mind.

"It looks great on you."

I thanked her for the shirt and told her I thought coffee was a great idea but I was buying. She agreed. I found a pen and wrote a quick note to Little Gene on a paper bag:

Thanks for everything, Little Gene! You're good people. I'll tell Miss October you said hi.
~Levi

We got out and I locked up the rig, left the key inside. Little Gene had another one. I smacked the side of the rig when I left, like the rugged old men in the movies, telling the driver to go on ahead. We're done here.

Drive safe, Little Gene.

***

We walked to a cafe away from the strip. It was my turn to get the stares—the raised eyebrows and slack jaws. We sat in a booth against the window in front and ordered coffee, then lit up smokes and talked.

"So, what are you going to major in?" I asked.

"Psychology. I want to be a social worker, maybe a child psychologist. Fix everything my asshole brother botches. Yin and Yang and all that."

"Yeah, you guys don't seem anything alike."

"Trust me, we're not. But he's only my half brother, and even that I question."

"I think you'll make a great psychologist."

"Thank you, Levi...Hey, I have to use the payphone real quick. Save my seat."

Starr went to the other side of the cafe, searched her pockets for a quarter and made a phone call that lasted all of thirty seconds, then came back and sat down.

"I have one more gift on the way."

At this point I'm becoming uncomfortable with the gifts and I tell her so.

Her face was stern, almost angry. "You know what I think? I think you've been shit on so much you think you're undeserving. You've gotta get out of that mindset."

All I could think of was that sometime in the near future the world was going to have one hell of a social worker.

Our coffee came and Starr talked about how she hoped to move to Seattle after school. She said she loved rain and it made her feel in touch with herself under all those clouds. She said she lived there briefly with her grandmother. Then her grandmother passed and she was forced to move to San Francisco to live with her mom and that she'd never go back there again. Too many bad memories, same as Vegas.

After we got seconds on the coffee, Starr looked out the window, smiled and said, "Here comes your other gift."

I followed her eyes and saw her brother, Tommy, reach for the cafe door and enter.

"Why is he here?"

"He's your ride." She put her hand up to stop me from speaking and said, "He's leaving for L.A. this morning, that's right outside Hermosa. You've got nothing to worry about. I've still got that picture and we made a deal. He lets you ride shotgun to L.A. and I get rid of the picture. You don't have to be friends. You don't have to say a word. Just sit there and think about Hermosa and how you'll be there before the day's over."

Tommy eyed the café, looking for us.

"Before the day's over?"

"Yeah. You're like four, maybe five hours away."

My chest tightened—excitement, fear, maybe a little doubt.

"You nervous?"

"I am."

"What's the worst that could happen?"

I thought about what Little Gene said about worst-case scenarios and speaking them out loud.

"That I never find him."

"*And* that you're not stuck at the foster home."

"Either way, I'm not riding with your brother. No way."

"I'm telling you, Levi. He's got everything to lose. That picture will do more damage than you think. He's not gonna touch you. Please just trust me."

Tommy spotted us, came over and sat next to Starr.

"Listen, dude. I'm sorry. I was wasted last night. My friends were egging me on. I shouldn't have done that."

"His name is Levi," Starr said.

"Sorry, Levi."

I didn't say anything, just sat and stared. My fists were balled, nails digging into my palms. I wanted to hit him. Starr tapped my foot under the table and mouthed the word "please," her eyes pleading.

"So you're leaving for L.A. and you're taking me with you?"

"Yep. Starr says you're headed for Hermosa. That's like half an hour from where I'm headed."

I hated that he knew where I was going, that he knew anything about me at all.

"Levi's got big plans there."

She meant well.

"You ready to head out?" Tommy flipped his keyring on his finger and into the palm of his hand.

"Now?" Starr asked.

"Well yeah. I'm hosting at my place tonight, lots of cleaning to do still. Plus, I've gotta hit the store, and I was hoping to squeeze in a run."

"Go run now."

"In Vegas? Yeah right. We doing this or what?"

Starr reached her hands across the table toward me, palms face up. I put my hands in hers, reluctantly.

"The hell is this?" Tommy scowled.

"Go wait in the car, Tommy. He'll be out in a minute."

"Okay, but I'm not waitin' long."

"You'll wait as long as I say," she said.

Tommy stormed off outside and got into a red convertible. The top was down. If he wasn't such a dick it might look good on him.

Starr and I held hands across the table and she thanked me for keeping her company and said she hopes I find what I'm looking for. She reached in her back pocket and handed me the picture she'd taken the night before. There I was, huddled on the ground with Tommy's foot held back, winding up for a kick to my ribs. If you were ever going to use a picture for discriminating evidence, it was a good one.

"Take this. Burn it, tear it up, whatever. I know you don't want anyone seeing this."

I took the picture. We stood up and hugged, then she kissed my forehead.

"You're gonna do great, Levi. Don't ever doubt yourself."

I told her the same and thanked her for everything. I paid for our coffee and left a dollar tip, then joined Tommy in a car he didn't deserve. He peeled away—billowing smoke, screeching tires.

Douchebag.

As we drove away, I realized the car was the nicest one I'd ever been in, with someone I hated behind the wheel, and I wondered if this was a little how Starr felt every night.

49 - At a Dangerous Pace

Once we were out of sight of the cafe, I told Tommy to stop the car. I never had any intention on riding with him to L.A. It was a nice gesture on Starr's part, but I'd made it this far. I'd get another ride. Or walk if I had to.

"No way, dude. You're sitting right there until we get to L.A. I won't be cut off because of your freak ass."

He sped up, ran a red light, then hit the freeway going close to seventy.

I told him I had the picture, said that nobody would find out. I dug it out of my back pocket, showed it to him.

"No way. There's probably more than one. I stop the car, you make a run for it, hitch to the nearest payphone, call my sister's hotel and tell her I left you in the desert. Next thing I know, Mom's got a photo in the mail and my shit is cut off. Hell no!"

He drove faster as he spoke. I went ahead and let him think whatever bullshit he wanted to. And for the next half hour we sat in silence while his foot kept us at a dangerous pace.

50 - Erasing the Past

We listened to the radio—some shit station that played butt rock. KISS came on once but it was new KISS and I wasn't interested. Music written without Ace, without Peter, when they betrayed us all and traded makeup for sequins and lace.

"So did you screw my sister or what?"

Half an hour of silence and that's what the prick opens with.

"Since when do you worry about who's sleeping with your sister?"

"Because if she's sleepin' with someone like you then I *know* something's wrong."

"There *is* something wrong...your sister's back there whoring herself out to pay for college while you get a free ride from Mommy."

Tommy slowed the car, then stopped. "Give me the picture and get the hell out!"

I jumped over the door and took off running, away from the road, fetching the matches from my pocket.

"You little prick!" Tommy yelled from behind.

Before he got to me, I lit a match and stuck the flame under the photo. Tommy caught up and we both watched the picture burn. I dropped it on the ground and the fire ate it. It didn't exist anymore.

"What'd you do that for?"

I didn't answer, just headed for the road. Tommy mumbled some bullshit, then headed back to his car, speeding past me with his middle finger in the air.

51 - Like a Treadmill

I was surrounded by nothing. No street signs, no trees, no shithole diners or single-pump stations. Not even a tumbleweed. I knew it'd be a long day. My chance at getting a ride was slim. The sun had yet to peak. But it would. And then the temp would drop once the sun did. I was thankful for the food, but without a single thing to drink I may as well have an empty backpack, which wouldn't have been so bad. The shit was getting heavy.

Going through the desert on foot feels like walking on a treadmill. There's no progression. The scenery never changes. It's mind numbing.

The coffee ran through me and I emptied on the side of the road, then sat down and wrote. There was a lot to write about. In the first hour, four cars passed. More than I thought there'd be. But I still had no ride and the sun was rising to an intimidating position. Each time a car passed, I stood with my thumb out. A surreal moment in the desert for passersby, I suppose. I took to walking again, that treadmill experience. But this time I focused on a landmark, like a rock up ahead, then celebrated each mark I passed. It kept me going.

One of the landmarks turned out to be an armadillo, its body partially flattened. I wondered if Tommy was the one who hit it and made up my mind it was.

52 - California Crossing

Hours passed. The scenery the same: A wasteland with a thick black vein that led to nowhere. I could see why Tommy chose the route. He could go as fast as he wanted. No fear of traffic. No fear of Johnny Law.

I checked my map more than once. Nothing. Though the state did have the courtesy of letting me know when I entered California by way of a welcome sign that stuck out like an evergreen splinter on a snake's belly. Passing that sign reminded me of the day I turned thirteen. Sister Jude asked if I felt different now that I was a teenager. I didn't.

That's how crossing into California felt.

53 - Disney Sand

Thirty-two cars passed before the sun fell. I could barely make out a small building ahead. No lights. It was a gas station—still functioning—with a shed in back. Being hungry is one thing. It doesn't feel good, and your gut reminds you often of the neglect. But being thirsty is on a different level. It's unforgiving. Ravenous. So when I spotted the half empty Coke on the brick sill of the station, I didn't hesitate. I just plugged it with my tongue and took sips, being careful not to catch the cigarette butt inside.

I savored the Coke, saved some to wash down a bag of chips and some jerky. I could see a small cooler inside the store, and if I wouldn't have found the Coke I think I would have busted through the window and charged the cooler. I told you. Ravenous.

I made a small fire behind the shed and slept on the ground. I kept the fire going as long as I could with a few wooden pallets and some signposts. It kept me warm enough to fall asleep, then burned out before dawn. The rest of the morning I flirted with sleep but we never really got acquainted again. I regretted not making the best of my ride to L.A. and had a hard time telling if I was full of pride or dignity. I sided with dignity.

***

I never even heard the truck pull in. Just before dawn the gas station owner showed up. I heard him tossing stuff around in the shed. I scrambled to my feet and hid against the back of it. When I bumped into a stack of hubcaps, things in the shed got quiet.

Then I heard the sound of shuffling feet. I stood frozen against the shed and stared out across the desert, entranced by the orange-purple glow of the sun as it woke California.

"What the...?" A man in his sixties or so stood dressed in dirty overalls with a patch that read *Gregory* written in cursive, a socket wrench in his hand. He pointed it at me and asked if I stole his pallets. I guess I kind of did.

"I'm sorry, sir. I burned them." I pointed to the circle of ash. "I burned your signposts too, sir."

He stared at the ash, trying to figure out what the hell.

"You burned them?"

"I'm sorry, sir. I was cold. I was dead thirsty too, but I didn't break into your store."

"Ha! Good luck with that. That shit's bulletproof."

It wasn't. Hell, the door's window had more than a few cracks, with a small piece in the corner gone altogether. A firm tap of the knuckles would have shattered the rest. I'd thought about it.

We traded stares. I think we were both deciding what to do. Me running, him swinging the wrench.

"I was saving those pallets to build a sandbox for the kids that come out...and the posts, those were for advertising and such. I figure you cost me some money. Forty bucks oughta cover it."

He held out his hand. I told the guy I had seventy-five cents and I was only passing through.

"Looks like you'll be workin' it off then. You can start by scattering that mess you made of my wood, then meet me inside and we'll get you something to drink. I can see the desert got to ya, melted your damn face right the hell away." He turned and left.

I kicked the remains of the fire about, mixing it in with the dirt, then grabbed my pack and ran to the store. The lights were on, the CLOSED sign flipped to OPEN. Gregory was inside and behind the register, sliding a drawer into it.

"Here ya go." He slammed a milk jug full of water onto the counter. I uncapped it quick-like and took to guzzling. "Woah, hey! If you're gonna make a mess take it outside." The front of my shirt was soaked, a growing puddle around my feet.

I told him I was sorry and asked if he had a mop. He did. I cleaned up the floor.

"You'll be running the pump today. Any tips you make go straight to me. In between customers you'll be cleaning out the cooler and you may as well mop the rest of the floor. I'll cook a frozen pizza at 1:00 and we'll split it. If you got something in that bag of yours for breakfast you best eat it now. You've got ten minutes."

I took the jug of water and headed outside, sat on the ground and ate as many donuts as I could.

We had four customers by 9:00 a.m., every one of them for gas. Gregory showed me how to work the pump, but he kept me clear of the register. He didn't trust me and I didn't blame him. With every car that stopped, I wanted to ask for a ride, get the hell to civilization. But I wanted to right the wrong and pay for the wood.

At 1:00 sharp, Gregory had the pizza cooked, cut, and served. We sat in the back of his truck and ate it. He told me he was building an amusement park on the land and it all started with the sandboxes.

"What you want to do see, is you wanna get the kid's attention. You get *their* attention, then you got their parent's attention. Ever seen a kid in the cereal aisle at a supermarket? It's a damn wrestlin' match. The kids kickin' and screamin' about needing this box of cereal and that box of cereal. You get a kid out here sees that sandbox, he'll go apeshit. The next thing you know, the parents are forking over cold hard cash for time in the sandbox.

"The key is a mascot. Just like them cereal boxes all got their cartoony characters on 'em, I'll be doin' the same. Every ride will have its own character. The sandbox has its share of ants, so I've drawn some mockups for that one. Next will come the swings. I've got a guy inside Crenshaw lookin' into that for me. These parents will want nothing more than to stretch their legs, grab some gas and shoo their screaming kids away to Gregory's Gayland. I haven't trademarked it yet. My guy in Crenshaw said gay don't mean happy no more. Still, I figure come end of summer I'll have my box and a set of swings. It's a start."

We finished the pizza and Gregory had me wipe down the pump and sweep the front. Even though the front was dirt. He said there's dirty dirt and then there's clean dirt. He wanted clean dirt.

Around 4:00 I asked Gregory when he closed. He said not until 9:00 but not to worry, that he'd give me a ride into town. And he did. I helped him close up the gas station, gave him the ten bucks I'd made in tips, and we headed west. He dropped me off in the middle of a small town and told me he hoped I learned a lesson.

I did. I learned I was a magnet for batshit crazy.

54 - Junkyard Dog

Things started feeling like California. It wasn't all palm trees and beaches yet, but the brown hilly terrain hinted at their arrival. That same hilly terrain found in the background of so many modern films. If Gramm Jones ever did one good thing on earth it was to allow a VCR in the rec room. I'll give them that.

***

It started to look like I wouldn't find a bed for the night, any place to crash. But then I ran across a junkyard full of cars with a hole in the fence held together by coat hangers. I loosened the hangers and squeezed through. I spotted a dog right away on the far end of the yard but he was chained up. I climbed a stack of cars and found the bed of an old Ford truck at the top and climbed in. I could see most of the yard from there, including a few workers hanging around. They were drinking beer and playing cards on a makeshift table in a large, open garage.

The moon shone on the cars, reflecting off side-view mirrors. Mountains of rusted coal packed with glistening diamonds. I watched the dog pace along the path he'd made, occasionally dip into his dishes, and tag anything he could reach. He finally laid down and I did too, using a bag of chips for a pillow.

55 - Big Dreams, Little Minds

I woke up before the sun. It made for a good time to leave. I did my best to seal up the hole in the fence, then walked down the road and ate what was left of the donuts. Except for the jerky, most of the food was crushed now, like the last bowl in a box of cereal. Crumbs and dust.

I checked my map and headed southwest. Only two cars passed by before I got a ride. They were newlyweds. Cans and streamers running behind the car, soap on the windows. The works. They were all smiles and wore nothing but bathing suits. I asked them why they had stopped to pick me up, they should be celebrating, getting away from it all. They told me they'd been married for ten years, that they'd renewed their vows after multiple affairs and were dedicating their lives to serving others and I was their first opportunity. They seemed very much in love. Laughing, smiling, flirting. At one point the woman reached into the man's lap as he drove, her arm moving up and down vigorously across the seat. I kept my gaze out the window, pretending not to notice. Then they lit up smokes and I did too.

"We're headed to Hollywood, Levi. My wife is going to pursue an acting career, with me as her agent." He put his arm around her. "Remember her face, because you're about to see it on every billboard and cover of every magazine from here to New York. She's got it!"

The man hooted and hollered, then his wife got excited and flashed her tits at him.

"You ridin' all the way with us, Levi? To Hollywood?"

"If you don't mind," I said.

"You may wanna keep your eyes back there because things might get busy up front if you know what I mean. We're newlyweds you know."

I don't think I ever looked in their direction again. When I wasn't looking out my window, I was thumbing through the Boy Scout book and thinking about Rainbow Rick and that beautiful bookstore of his. God rest his soul.

The Boy Scouts seemed like a cool enough idea, earning badges and what not. Little accomplishments. Learning about nature and survival. But damned if you'd ever catch me in that scarf.

Keeping to myself, my eyes off the front, was about the time I wished I had a Walkman. A kid at Gramm Jones had one, always in his own little world, vegging out to his tunes, rocking in a chair for hours. He'd wear the batteries out in one sitting if they let him.

***

We made a pit stop and the newlyweds bought me a Coke and a sandwich. I ate mine in the car while they went to the bathroom. They were in there for a while and when they came out they giggled a lot and smelled like fish cooked in mushrooms.

***

Over time, the cans behind the car became fewer, the noise lessoned, and the traffic began to congest. Even more than Denver. And as the view changed from brown hills peppered with green to valleys full of civilization, I was in a movie. Mom and Dad driving me to our new home in Beverly Hills. The house where I'd throw parties while the parents were away, and shenanigans would commence. And Levi the skullface boy would be the only one who could take his new school to the state championship in a variety of sports, where the jock-types both admired and envied him and his chiseled jaw and surfing prowess.

***

The groom drove slowly through Los Angeles while the bride looked at a small map of the city. They had circled different areas with a red pen.

"Have you ever heard of Sunset Boulevard, Levi?"

I had.

"That's our first stop. We'll drop you off there if it's okay. We'll be heading to the Hollywood sign to consummate the area, get some stardom juices flowing." They giggled like children who'd just shared a taboo first kiss.

I told them Sunset was fine, and they thanked me for allowing them to help me, then held hands between the seats.

***

L.A. was filled with people. Tadpoles in a puddle. Walking, riding bikes, rollerskating, and more than a few camped under canopies strategically placed in parks and building alcoves. The problem with homelessness was evident right away. But if you were going to be homeless, L.A. seemed like a best-case scenario. Like a little community of the lost and alone with enough area to panhandle and enough dumpsters to pillage without stepping on toes.

I began to wonder if the city caused the homeless or if it was a magnet for them. Was L.A. a place where dreams died or gave birth to them? Did L.A. tease the impossible, presenting the bigtime as attainable for anyone with a desire? Were the canopies filled with broken dreams that began with nothing more than delusion? Or did L.A. cause the delusional? And would the horny couple in front end up on the streets, covered with cardboard to hide their bathing-suited bodies during cold nights?

The chicken or the egg?

"This should do it, Levi," the groom said.

They dropped me off and drove away. A single streamer held on to the bumper by a large piece of duct tape, the soap across the back window read "Just Mareed".

Big dreams, little minds. I hoped they made it.

56- Dangerous & Attractive

I found myself in a cluster of strip malls, tightly packed businesses. The street was pregnant with them. Within a stone's throw, I could get a massage, eat Mexican, eat pizza, get my palm read, stop for gas, then go have my teeth cleaned next to a motel with bars over its windows. It was dangerous and attractive all at once. A chaotic madhouse full of too many choices. Perfect.

57 - If You Got the Dime

I toyed with the idea of staying in L.A. for the day, taking an on-foot tour of Hollywood highlights, but with being only twenty miles from Hermosa and the entire day ahead, it made little sense to do anything but head for the beach.

I stopped at a bus stop bench and checked my map, had a smoke. I looked for the closest freeway. Nobody picks up hitchers in the city, or the urban areas. That's like trying to sell sand in the desert or sunscreen to an Eskimo. People need to see you're going somewhere. They need to see you're stuck between A and B before they'll consider you.

Sunset Boulevard was appealing. Lots of T & A. Lots of metalheads. I had to wonder how many legitimate stars I had passed on the street without knowing it. I saw a man window shopping, bags in hand from various stores. He had on a baseball cap and shades. He thought he was disguised. I stopped and asked for his autograph. I didn't know who he was. He set his stuff down and got a marker from his back pocket. Like a jackknife, always there in case it's needed. I had him sign the check pad Lucille gave me. He signed it *"Levi, Catch some tasty waves & you'll be fine."* His name was a scribbled mess that I couldn't make out. But he was a star. He'd made it.

***

I decided I'd walk to Hermosa. I figured I could make it there by sundown, no problem. It would give me plenty of time to think, to plan. To prepare. I filled up on chips and the rest of the jerky. A guy in Burger King charged me ten cents for a water. I got a large, filled it mostly with ice so it'd melt on the way.

Ten cents for water. Bullshit.

58 - Clean Jeans

According to the digital clock above the bank in Hermosa, it took me almost seven hours to get there. That includes a few breaks along the way. After the second break I nearly stuck my thumb out. I'd put my miles on these feet. And young or not, junk food doesn't put a kick in your step. I felt lethargic, drained. But as I saw the approaching cross streets and matched them with the map, I hit a second wind. Pure adrenaline. I was at a finish line. I pictured the man who looked like me waiting there, water in hand and a story to tell on how the hell I ended up in Gramm Jones. But it wasn't like that. My greeting was a group of skateboarders sipping on Mountain Dew, butts on boards, asking if I had an extra smoke. I did. They didn't give me any shit. No questions. No jokes. Just a "thanks, bro" as I tossed them a cigarette.

I had sixty-five cents left and was running out of food. I started taking note of dumpsters for after dark. I couldn't hop in during the day anymore. Dignity. Pride. One of those.

Really, my mind was on the beach itself, where Sister Jude said she'd seen him. I never asked how long ago it was. Sister Jude couldn't have been more than thirty-five now. She said she was around ten when she saw him. How old was he at the time? A teenager? An adult? I crunched numbers using different scenarios, speculating his age then and now. I didn't want anything to do with any number that reflected old age. Or death. I was getting anxious. I had to stop. I'd head to the beach soon, take a look, maybe ask around.

***

I needed a shower. It'd been eleven days. Starr's musky perfume had worn off the shirt and I could smell my jeans every time I sat down. I'd seen in a movie once where a guy took his clothes off and washed them at a laundromat, sat there in his underwear while his clothes went through the cycles. I went back and asked the skaters where the closest laundromat was. Half a mile down the road, on the right. I asked them if they surfed at all.

"Nah, we stick to the street, sometimes vert," a kid with long blonde hair said, his wrists covered in clanging bracelets, a bandana on his head. "Got a deck? You can join us. We're headed to McKinley."

Kids being decent to me. Not something I was used to. I told him thanks, maybe some other time and gave them another smoke.

***

The laundromat sat on the corner next to a hair salon and an arcade. Two people were inside.

One reading a book, the other finishing off some vending machine food. I checked the washers. I had enough for a small load as long as I bought no detergent. And I was a dime short for the dryer. I stuck my finger in the payphone coin returns. Nothing.

    I went to the back of the 'mat and took my pants off, tossed them in the wash and started the load. Found a newspaper and covered my lap, then sat with *Some Kind of Hero* for the next twenty minutes. As far as anyone knew, I was wearing shorts.

***

    The load finished and I put my jeans on, soaking wet. But they were clean. As clean as water could get them. I hit a taco stand, got another cup of water. It was free. Then I hit the street and sat in the sun under a palm tree. I wrote and let my pants dry. I was stalling.

Chapter 59 - Shitting Back

After too much debate, I checked my map and headed toward the water. The edge of the world. The last week and a half felt like a lifetime. I'd packed more adventure, life lessons, and experience in that short time than sixteen years at Gramm Jones. I realized I'd rather be homeless, eating trash and sleeping in bushes and learning about life, about humanity—the good and the bad—than spend another night in that Colorado cage. Every bully that stepped foot in that place I no longer blamed. Gramm Jones made them who they are. Like prison does for some. You get caught making a stupid decision while under the influence of the wrong crowd—toting a bag of weed, lifting a bottle of booze from the store, or taking a swing at the wrong person—you go to jail with regret and a lesson learned, and you walk out a criminal. But give every one of those kids at Gramm Jones the kind of freedom I have now and you're going to see a different side of them. The world shit on them. Now they're shitting back. It's all they know.

60 - Doc's Boy

I stopped reading street signs, stopped checking my map. I was where I needed to be. I found a road with more of the same shops Sunset had to offer but catering more to the counterculture: Skate shops, bike shops, tattoo parlors, clubs, and record stores. I spotted a small bookstore but didn't stop. The ocean was up ahead. I could smell it. The road peaked, then dropped, and up ahead was the beach, then a vast expanse of blue. My knees grew weak and I had to sit. I copped a squat on a cement wall and finished off the last bag of chips, my eyes glued to the ocean. I'd seen photographs, calendars, posters. But this wasn't still and silent. This was alive. Moving. Forever kissing the beach with calm, and sometimes violent, waves. The beach held readers, nappers, sunbathers, runners, surfers and observers in deep thought and meditation. Worshipers and partakers.

This was my new home, with or without a room to call my own. With or without a bed. This was who I am.

If I were you, I'd learn to surf.

I planned on it.

I watched the beach closely, looking for him. Long hair with a bone face. An hour passed and I gave up for the day, headed back up the hill toward the shops. A man was scurrying outside a

T-shirt shop, tearing down displays and taking them inside. He had signs out, tables set up with shirts, stickers and posters for sale. He saw me and waved me over.

"Hey, kid. I'm in the middle of closing up for the day but I gotta catch the bank before it closes. Can you watch the tables while I make a deposit? Will only take me a minute."

"Sure," I said.

"Thanks, man. I'll toss you a shirt when I get back."

He ran down the street to a bank on the corner. I finished what the guy had started, stacked the shirts and took them inside, as well as the posters and the stickers, then broke down the tables and carried those in. By the time I was done the guy was back.

"Hell, you didn't have to do all that."

I told him sitting there for a few minutes wasn't worth a shirt. I was glad to do it.

"Pick one out." He pointed to the shirts.

I already had my eye on one—aqua blue with a big orange sun, a surfer catching waves in front of it. It said Ocean Pacific under his board.

"Nice choice," he said. "You ride?"

"No."

"Hell, that's surprising. You're Doc's boy, right?"

My throat dried, my heart raced.

"Who?"

"Doc...guy that owns the surf shop down the hill, around the corner. That's not your old man?'

I stared off, shook my head. It was a slow no, too subtle to notice. He saw my backpack and asked a different question.

"You're not from around here, are you?"

I shook my head again, visibly.

"All's I'm gonna say is you may wanna head down to *Doc's Surf & Wax*.

"I will, thanks." It was hard to keep my cool.

"Listen. I run this sale out here on the walk every day. I could use a body here keeping an eye on things while I paint the store. Just for a few days. You ever run a register before?"

"No."

"Good. I don't use one. I write it all down on these pads here." He pointed toward a glass counter, a small pad of receipts sat on top. "You good with math? I mean...you can hand out some change, right?"

I told him I could.

"Wanna give it a go? Say 8:00 a.m. tomorrow?"

My first day at Hermosa and I was being offered a job. Near the ocean. I told him I'd be happy to and that I'd see him early tomorrow but right now I had to be somewhere. My mind was on fire. We shook hands, exchanged names and I walked out of *The T-Shirt Emporium* with a job and a lump in my throat, thinking of the guy down the hill.

He was still alive. He was here.

61 - Like the Moon

I ran down the street, stood at the top of the hill and wondered if I was Doc's worst nightmare. Something he left in the past and wanted kept that way. Or was I the product of late sixties promiscuity, disposed of by the one who carried me, the father never having known. It was the former that scared the shit out of me.

"The worst-case scenario is he rejects me and I live on the beach. My beautiful new home." I said it out loud.

With my pants nearly dry, I went down the hill toward the beach, dodging bikes and skateboards, signs and light posts. The street hung left. More shops. I crossed the street and looked at the shop signs behind me. A half block down, a large surfboard hung above an awning. The surfboard read *"Doc's Surf & Wax"* in blue, wavy letters.

I walked further still but kept my distance and hid behind a palm tree in the sand. The shop's door was open. I stood and watched as people went in and out of the shop. Some walked in with boards, some without. There was a lot of traffic through those doors. A lot of business.

An old man, drunk as shit, snuck up behind me and asked if this was the line. I told him there was no line here, that I was just waiting for someone. He said, "Is it okay if I cut then? I've gotta piss like you wouldn't believe." I told him to go ahead. He pulled his pants down to his ankles and peed on the tree, bare ass. Then he left toward the beach.

I looked back at *Doc's Surf & Wax*, and there stood a man, closing up shop. A sun-bleached ponytail resting on his back, bright orange shirt, knee-length shorts, and skin that held decades of the sun's rays. I watched as he toyed with his keys, then locked the door. There was a surfboard propped against the building, and when he turned to grab it, his face shone like the moon.

Brilliant white bone.

62 - Life's a Beach

I didn't come out from behind the tree. Not for a while. I hid, unable to breathe. And when I looked again, the guy was gone.

I wandered on the beach, taking note of landmarks so I wouldn't get lost. I had work in the morning. I was out of food but had no appetite. My nerves were shot, and I could think of nothing else but Doc.

***

After dark, I stripped naked and went swimming. My first time in the ocean. The water was perfect. I scrubbed my pits, my junk, my ass. Then I soaked my KISS shirt and socks and put my new surfer shirt on. I hadn't realized until I took my shoes off that I could use some new ones. They reeked of too many miles.

The beach went on forever. An endless sandbox. I thought of Gregory and his dreams for Gayland and wondered if he'd ever even seen the shore, if he'd ever even seen an amusement park. Big dreams, little mind.

***

I camped against the wall that separated the street from the beach and slept there hidden from traffic, from shop owners. From Doc. The sand made for a decent mattress, and the distant sound of the ocean lulled me to sleep. I dreamt of surfing under the stars, the moon lighting my way as I crashed into the arms of California.

Look at me now, Sister Jude.

63 - Prepared to Work

I woke up with the sun, the beach already littered with meditators and runners. My appetite had come back. I was starving and regretted not hitting a dumpster the night before, but it's hard digging through garbage without being driven by hunger pangs.

I wrote a little, then walked the beach some, asked a runner for the time. 6:20. I walked a pier and watched a young boy fish, his pole bigger than him. He hadn't caught anything yet, but even at his age he seemed to appreciate the peace the ocean brought. As it crept closer to 8:00 I made my way toward *The T-Shirt Emporium*, made a quick stop in front of *Doc's Surf & Wax*. It wasn't open yet. I sat on the wall across the street and watched the shop, flipped through the Boy Scout book.

As I put my book away and prepared to leave, Doc showed up, board under his arm. His hair wasn't in a ponytail this time. It rested on his shoulders, fell down his back. He was barefoot and wore a different pair of shorts—bright blue—and an open white shirt showing his tone build. He looked as cool as I ever wanted to.

I waited until he was inside, then ran up the street to the T-shirt shop, hungry as shit but prepared to work.

64 - Bones Brigade

"Morning, Levi!"

"Good morning, Dan."

"I stop by the bakery every morning, got a few extra today. Wasn't sure if pastries is your thing, but help yourself." He pointed to the glass counter where a cardboard box sat on top, open. "There's a pot of coffee in the back in case that's your thing, too. Me? I can't see straight until I get a few cups in me."

I thanked him and pretended I wasn't as hungry as I was.

"We never talked about pay yesterday. How does four dollars an hour under the table sound?"

I wasn't sure what under the table meant, but I agreed. If I could make 15 bucks going across country last more than a week, then by the end of the day I figured I'd have at least a few week's worth of cash.

"Alright! Well, let me show you the ropes, then we'll set up outside and I'll get to painting. You're doing me a big favor here, Levi. I've been meaning to paint this place for a few years now. These kids like bright colors nowadays. Blues and pinks. Purples and Oranges. Lime green even. I got me some ideas. Check it out."

Dan handed me a magazine ad for sunglasses. The ad was full of overlapping triangles, circles, and squares, all Dayglo colors.

"I'm gonna throw some squigglies in there, too. Gotta keep up with the times."

I told him it was a great idea, that it'd look sharp once he was done.

While Dan went over the prices and how to fill out the receipts, I tried my best to focus, but my mind was on Doc. The thought of walking into his shop, him seeing me. I didn't want to reopen a closed wound, or be shunned by my own kind. I ran every bad scenario through my mind. I prepared for the worst.

"And that's pretty much it. You got any questions I'll be right in here."

I sat at the tables, organized the shirts, arranged the stickers, ate pastries and drank coffee. Business picked up as the hours went by. Everyone was nice to me, and Dan said I was doing a great job. I'd peek in the store every once in a while, check out his artwork. It was looking real good and just like the ad.

Just before noon, a young girl came up—scrawny, long brown hair, couldn't have been more than five or six, a real inquisitive type. She played with her hair nervously, poking her finger with the ends of it. She asked me my name and we started talking. She had questions about each shirt, each sticker. What they meant and what they said. I had a hard time answering. I couldn't tell which were bands and which were brands. We went through the stickers together, one at a time. She pointed to one with four black bars on it. I didn't know. She pointed to another that said Circle Jerks. I quickly buried it under the others and directed her attention elsewhere. She asked about a Yin Yang symbol. I told her I wasn't sure but that life has a way of balancing itself out, the good and the bad, and I thought that's what the symbol meant.

Then she pointed to a sticker and said, "I want that one." It had a skeleton on it, poking his head through a hole. It said Bones Brigade. She asked me what it said and I told her.

"What does brigade mean?"

I told her I thought it meant a small group of something, like soldiers. She said "Like you and Doc? Are you the bones brigade?"

I didn't answer. I couldn't.

"How much?"

"Seventy-five cents."

"I want it," she said.

I wrote up a receipt and took the money, then she handed me the sticker. "I want you to have it." It was a sweet gesture, one that crushed me. She patted my hand and said "I'll see you around, Levi!," then ran toward the beach.

***

At noon, Dan went and got us subs and told me to take an hour lunch. He asked if while I was out would I run down to the beach and take a flier to lifeguard tower #19.

"You'll see the number painted on the back. My buddy, Chuck, that's his post. Just tell him I sent you and give him the flier. He'll hang it for us."

Dan handed me the flier. It was for an upcoming sale: Twenty percent off all shirts this coming weekend.

"I'll be done painting by then, but if you're around I could use your help during the sale. It can get pretty busy around here."

I told him sure thing, I'd be there.

I took my sub and the flier and headed toward the beach. At the bottom of the hill I turned left. This time I didn't cross the street. I stayed on the same side as Doc's shop. I was going for a closer look. The sound of waves and chatter and seagulls carried on in the background, but I didn't hear them. I shut the world out. As I drew closer, I was focused on the door of *Doc's Surf & Wax*, afraid he'd come out and see me. Shun me. I got close enough to see the door was closed, with a note attached:

Closed for lunch, back in an hour. Catch them waves!

Relieved, sort of, I crossed the street and hit the beach. Tower #19 was easy to find. Chuck seemed cool enough and posted the flier while I was there. He told me that I'm a lucky guy, that Dan wouldn't hire just anyone but he could see why he hired me. And he said "Your dad rules this beach, man. He's the raddest guy I know."

I didn't say anything, just nodded.

Chuck let me eat my sub on the tower ramp. I watched the surfers. It looked hard, staying on the board. I wasn't so sure I could do it, but eventually I was going to try. I said goodbye to Chuck and headed toward the shop. A Frisbee landed at my feet and I picked it up, tossed it to a guy with his hands in the air.

Then I saw Doc.

He was walking toward me, shirtless and dripping wet, board in his arms. His head was down and he didn't see me. But he would. I wanted to run, to hide my face. But I didn't move. I couldn't pussy out now. This was why I left Gramm Jones, why I slept on the ground and ate garbage, why I wore dog piss jeans and hitched rides with drunks and psychos and polygamists and delusional newlyweds.

And then he saw me.

He came to a dead stop in the sand. Time stood still, and every bad scenario I'd thought of earlier played out in my head. And I thought how every lonely kid like me has delusions too, our own little dreams about happiness and being loved. Dreams that often never come true. And I thought...this was one of those dreams.

Then Doc dropped his board and ran toward me, that rad long hair of his trailing behind. He slowed, stopped, and we stood toe to toe. Then he grabbed my arms and pulled me in, hugging me. His body shook against mine, subtle spasms as he gripped me tighter, cradling my head with one hand, squeezing my shoulder with the other. He pushed me back and held me at arm's length, looked me up and down, got a real good look at me. And I can't be sure, but I think he was probably smiling.

I know I was.

I Believe in Gratitude:

Thank you to my wife, Mary. My kids: Kristin Marie, Elijah Shine, and Nekoda Lee. John Boden, cover photographer Chas Bacon, my parents, the original Rainbow Rick, the unnamed strangers who gave me rides when hitchin', the abundance of synthwave, KISS, and Alice Cooper I digested while writing this book. My patrons: Shaun Hupp, Dan Padavona, Connie McNeil Bracke, Dyane Hendershot, Linda Lee, Michael Perez, Shannon Everyday, Steve Gracin, and Tim Feely. Black Flag, Ace Frehley, Stephen Graham Jones, J. David Osborne, Joe Lansdale, Raymond Carver, David Lynch, Buffalo Bill (sorry, man), Denver, Golden, Boulder, Coors, the 80s, and to you, the reader.

Author note:

While I've never lived in a foster home and I don't have a skull for a face, some of this book is autobiographical. I'll let you decide which parts. Oh, and if you ever make it to Lookout Mountain, tell Buffalo Bill I'm sorry. He'll know.

Author Bio

Chad lives in Battle Creek, MI. with his wife, children. For over two decades, he has been a contributor to several different outlets in the independent music and film scene, offering articles, reviews, and artwork. He has written for *Famous Monsters of Filmland, Rue Morgue, Cemetery Dance*, and *Scream* magazine. His fiction can be found in a few dozen magazines and anthologies including his own 18-story collection *NIGHT AS A CATALYST*. Lutzke is known for his heartfelt dark fiction and deep character portrayals. In the summer of 2016 he released his dark coming-of-age novella *OF FOSTER HOMES AND FLIES* which has been praised by authors Jack Ketchum, James Newman, John Boden, and many others. Later in 2016 Lutzke released his contribution to bestselling author J. Thorn's *AMERICAN DEMON HUNTERS* series, and 2017 saw the release of his novella *WALLFLOWER*. His latest, *STIRRING THE SHEETS*, was published by Bloodshot Books in spring 2018. Halloween 2018 his novella OUT BEHIND THE BARN co-written with author John Boden will be published by Shadow Work Publishing.

A neglected 12-year-old boy does nothing to report the death of his mother in order to compete in a spelling bee. A tragic coming-of-age tale of horror and drama in the setting of a hot New Orleans summer.

"Original, touching coming of age."
    ~Jack Ketchum, author of THE GIRL NEXT DOOR

"Disturbing, often gruesome, yet poignant at the same time, Chad Lutzke's

OF FOSTER HOMES AND FLIES is one of the best dark coming-of-age tales I've read in years. You'll laugh (sometimes when you know you shouldn't), you'll cry, you'll find yourself wondering how soon you can read more of this guy's work. Highly recommended!"
~ James Newman, author of MIDNIGHT RAIN, ODD MAN OUT, and THE WICKED

"With OF FOSTER HOMES AND FLIES, Lutzke is firing on all cylinders. It's a lean mean emotional machine. Coming-of-age presented in a fresh direction. Bearing tremendous emotional weight and heart. It made me cry. "
~John Boden, author of JEDI SUMMER.

"OF FOSTER HOMES AND FLIES by Chad Lutzke is a lovely addition to the coming of age subgenre. He creates in the character of Denny an authentic young man with passions and foibles, someone easy to relate to and root for. The novella hits all the right notes you expect out of a coming of age tale, while also providing a plot that has originality and surprises."
~Mark Allan Gunnells, author of FLOWERS IN A DUMPSTER and WHERE THE DEAD GO TO DIE

"...one of those real treats that comes down the pipe and manages to get you all excited about reading again...the whole thing is just beautiful."
~ Ginger Nuts of Horror

"Of Foster Homes and Flies is the darkest, most disturbing story Chad Lutzke has written. It's also his best...the ultimate one-finger salute to oppression...Highly recommended."
~Dan Padavona, author of CRAWLSPACE, QUILT and STORBERRY

"...a brilliant coming of age story. This isn't your average horror book...a masterpiece."
~Horroraddicts.net

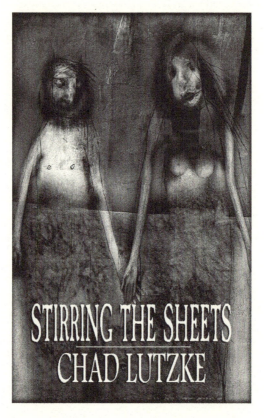

An elderly funeral home worker, struggling with the loss of his wife, develops an unnatural attraction to a corpse that resembles his late bride in her younger years. A story of morbid desperation, loneliness, and letting go.

"Stirring the Sheets is a disturbing tale of loss that both tugs at your heartstrings and turns your stomach."
 ~Zach Bohannon, bestselling author and co-owner of Molten Universe Media

" Lutzke writes of insurmountable grief as if it's an old acquaintance, drawing the audience into a story they can't put down. Heart wrenching and touching."

~ The Sisters of Slaughter, Bram Stoker Award nominees/authors of
MAYAN BLUE & THOSE WHO FOLLOW

"This blew me completely and utterly away...contains the entire spectral range of emotions. I guarantee you will feel them all."
~Nev Murray, Confessions of a Reviewer

"Bittersweet, full of sorrow, love, grace, and hope. A wonderful read with a twisted edge."
~Amber Fallon, author of THE WARBLERS

"Stirring the Sheets is a mesmerizing and believable tale of lost love and a broken protagonist...a haunting tale of a man come undone by grief. Lutzke has a keen grasp of the dark psychological elements of bereavement."
~Duncan Ralston, author of WOOM and SALVAGE

After an encounter with a homeless man, a high school graduate becomes obsessed with the idea of doing heroin, challenging himself to try it just once. A bleak tale of addiction, delusion, and flowers

"Lutzke creates a dark vision of a realistic horror. It's beautifully told and powerful..."
    ~Splatterpunk Zine

"It's gripping and tragic, and very excellently written."
    ~Mark Allan Gunnells, author of Where the Dead Go to Die

"...a novella rich in character development."
　～Char's Horror Corner

'Powerful. Moving. Bleak...A great book by a great author."
　～Shaun Hupp, author of Pound

"Chad gets inside the human existence, turns it inside out, and nails it to the wall."
　～Mark Matthews, author of Milk-Blood and Body of Christ

"Chad has a knack for writing believable, grounded characters dealing with honest problems, fears. Wallflowers is no exception."
　～Zachary Walters, The Eyes of Madness

"An absolute must read; well written and infinitely engaging."
　～James H. Longmore, author of Tenebrion

To join my VIP reader list and be included in all future giveaways, visit
www.chadlutzke.com